BOARDWALK QUEEN

JILLIAN FROST

BOARDWALK QUEEN

JILLIAN FROST

Also by Jillian Frost

Princes of Devil's Creek

Cruel Princes

Vicious Queen

Savage Knights

Battle King

Boardwalk Mafia

Boardwalk Kings

Boardwalk Queen

Boardwalk Reign

Devil's Creek Standalone Novels

The Darkest Prince

Wicked Union

For a complete list of books, visit JillianFrost.com.

BOARDWALK QUEEN

JILLIAN FROST

Epigraph

"There's three ways to do things, the right way, the wrong way,
and the way that I do it."

~ *Casino*

Chapter One

NICO

Hours before the dinner party...

Obligation sucked. Duty, family, honor, all things I had lived by for years, even before I understood the meaning of the words. So when my father ordered me to marry Vittoria Vitale, I couldn't refuse him.

He wasn't just my father.

Salvatore Luciano was the boss.

We gathered in the dining room at my father's penthouse with the entire Vitale family on one side and mine on the other. Even Paulie was here to witness the worst moment of my life. Well, the worst moment would have been marrying the ugly bitch.

It wouldn't come to that.

I hoped.

Vittoria sat beside her parents, with her brothers on her father's right. They called her oldest brother Greasy Joe, which wasn't because of all the product he wore in his dark hair.

He was a sneaky fuck.

Even his men didn't trust him.

He'd gotten the nickname in high school before becoming a

made man. Carlo, the asshole who'd given Angelo the scar on his right cheek, sat beside his older brother.

People started calling Angelo Little Scarface afterward. And my brother repaid Carlo by making a sex tape with his wife and sending it to him.

His wife kept sneaking glances at Angelo. Even though he'd only fucked her to get back at her husband, she still wanted his dick. She was married to an ugly bastard. All of the Vitales were varying degrees of grotesque.

I never thought we'd be peacefully sitting across the Vitales. Dante put a bullet in the wall right next to Carlo's head the last time we met like this. He hadn't forgiven them for what happened to Angelo. Dante was fiercely protective of the twins.

Before the Vitales got here, Dante pulled me aside and said, "You better fuck that bitch up good. Because if you don't, the three of us will."

My father stood at the head of the table, then tipped his head at me. He'd already given a toast and smoothed things over with the Vitales.

That was my cue.

I rose from the chair and removed the ring box from my pocket. Then, going through the motions I'd rehearsed, I walked to the other side of the table. My heart thumped, trying to claw its way out of my chest with each step I took toward Vittoria.

My heart wanted Ava.

Every part of me did.

I didn't want to do this.

Fuck.

I glanced over at my mother. She was in town with her dance group for a show at the Portofino. For a woman in her early fifties, she didn't look much older than me. But you would never know she had a son who was almost thirty years old.

Mom sat beside my dad in a gold dress that, paired with her blonde hair, made her look like she was glowing. My mother had a certain magnetism about her. A special something my father spotted the first time he saw her on stage.

2

She flashed a bright smile and tipped her head to encourage me. We'd spoken about the engagement when my dad handed me the ring. No one ever questioned my dad, not even her. If he believed this was the right thing to do, then so did she.

So did my brothers.

Angelo would have chopped Vittoria into pieces and sent her back to her brothers in a box. Dante would have gone a similar route. And Stefan would have tortured her daily to get revenge for his twin.

Dad knew what he was doing.

I wasn't going to hurt her.

Dropping to one knee beside Vittoria's chair, I felt like my throat was about to close up. I opened my mouth to speak, my tongue so dry I had to swallow.

Why was this so hard?

It wasn't nerves.

I had a steady hand and never faltered when I killed a man. I didn't think twice when I pulled the trigger.

But marriage?

Fuck, no.

Vittoria Vitale had long, dark hair that looked like she'd stuck her finger in an electrical outlet and then tried to tame the mess with gel. Even the makeup on her face didn't help enhance her features.

As Dante said, she was hideous.

Bruttissima.

I would never treat Vittoria like a wife. I'd never fuck her or have children with her.

I wanted Ava.

But the past was repeating itself.

To keep Ava in my life, she would have to play the same role as my mother and be my mistress. My dad loved and provided for her, but they couldn't marry.

Would Ava go for it?

I should have said something before I fucked her, but I wasn't ready to let her go.

She was mine.

On one knee beside Vittoria's chair, I opened the velvet box my father had shoved into my hand before they arrived. A ten-carat diamond that screamed, I have too much fucking money.

So I imagined Ava sitting before me as I said, "Will you marry me?"

Even when I slipped the ring onto Vittoria's meaty finger, I thought about my girl.

Was it love?

I wasn't sure.

It was something.

Obsession.

Possession.

I'd never felt any of those things with another woman. So that had to count for something. Every word I spoke to her was the truth. Ava knew the real Nicodemus Luciano, and I couldn't say anyone else did.

Only her.

After I proposed, we split into groups. My brothers were in the sitting room with my dad and the Vitale men. Mom kept the Vitale wives entertained in the kitchen, telling them stories about her years as a dancer. She was so good at bullshitting her way through these kinds of events.

It came naturally to her.

Me, not so much.

I stood outside the sitting room and scrolled through my cell phone, trying to find the courage to tell Ava about the engagement.

Heels clicked on the tiled floor, and Vittoria stood in front of me when I lifted my head. She curled her fingers around my wrist and tugged on my arm.

"Can I speak to you for a moment, Nicodemus?"

I glanced into the room at my father, who lit a cigar for Vincenzo. What a sight? They looked like old friends, drinking and smoking and telling war stories. I never thought I'd see the old man settle the score with the Vitales.

But what changed?

I still didn't understand his motives.

Neither did my brothers.

Was it to keep our enemies closer?

Angelo argued with Carlo in Italian, his voice rising a few octaves. His top lip curled up into a snarl like he was seconds from attacking. "Your wife likes taking it up the ass." A wicked cackle escaped his throat. "I can send you the video if you need a reminder." He got in Carlo's face, who was now standing nose-to-nose with my brother. "Do you think of me every time you fuck that whore?"

"I hear you got a sweet piece of pussy you're hiding in this hotel." Carlo gripped Angelo's tie. "Maybe I'll pay her a visit later."

Stefan laughed. "She wouldn't touch your limp dick."

"That's enough," Dad shouted. He pointed at the chair beside Stefan and tipped his head for Angelo to resume his place. "No more fighting. We're going to be a family."

"Fuck them," Angelo hissed.

"I second that," Stefan chimed.

Dante folded his arms over his chest and smirked.

"*Basta*," Dad yelled. "Sit."

Angelo's eyes flared as he looked at our father with a crazed expression.

Dad gritted his teeth. "I said sit, Angelo."

I couldn't wait for the wedding.

It would be a miracle if everyone in the bridal party weren't dead by the end of the reception. And if I had my way, we wouldn't get to that point. There was a better way to avoid war.

As Vincenzo intervened with Carlo, I took that as my cue to get the fuck out of here. I escorted Vittoria down the hall, so we could get some distance from family bonding time.

Before my brother egged on Carlo, my dad talked too loud and drank too much. He looked happy, content. Maybe it was because my mom was in town for the week. His mood suddenly shifted every time she was here.

Of course, my brothers hated it.

I stopped at the end of the corridor and leaned back against the wall. "What do you want to talk about?"

"The wedding." Vittoria folded her arms beneath her breasts, a hard stare plastered on her face. "I have my reservations about this marriage. I'm sure you can understand why."

"Our parents want us to marry." I stuffed my hands into my pockets. "I don't see the problem. This is standard practice for Mafia families."

"Yes." She pressed her lips into a thin line. "I'm well aware of what is normal for people like us. But I have concerns about this working between us."

"And why is that?"

"Because you have a bit of a reputation," she said with her nose tipped up like she was better than me. "I've heard the rumors. And I refuse to marry you if you're not planning to be faithful to me."

Like fucking hell I would ever be faithful to her. Vittoria would be my wife in name only. I was still trying to devise a strategy to get both of us out of the marriage.

Neither of us wanted this.

And I couldn't even imagine how Ava would take the news. She would be devastated. I was a coward for not telling her before we got into the shower this morning.

It was the least she deserved.

But with Ava, nothing was black and white. We still weren't sure if she would side with her father. And if she did, that would change everything between us.

"You have no reason to worry. I won't be unfaithful."

I was so good at lying it was like second nature. The only time I told the truth was when I was with Ava. Nothing was faked or forced with her. She knew me better than anyone else in this world.

She beamed with a smile that lit up her face. "Good. I'm glad we're on the same page."

Her father cheated on her mother. Even her brothers stepped

out on their wives. I wouldn't be here if my dad hadn't gone behind Guilia's back and slept with my mom.

Vittoria was either naive or stupid to think made men were saints. Whores let us do the nasty shit we wouldn't do with wives. Although, the more I thought about keeping Ava around long-term, the more I wanted one woman.

Vittoria flashed a pleased smile. "I should see what our mothers are up to in the kitchen. We'll talk soon about the wedding."

I stood in the same spot for several minutes after she walked away. My heart wouldn't stop racing, beating so loudly my ears rang. So I removed my cell phone from my pocket and flipped through the pictures. I took a few shots of Ava when she was sleeping. She looked so peaceful, so damn beautiful.

An hour later, the Vitales left my dad's penthouse, promising to return for dinner to announce the engagement in front of our friends and family.

I sat in the living room with my brothers. The twins were on each side of Dante, dressed in the same black Gucci suit. Except Angelo wore a gold tie and Stefan red. They drank from the glasses in their hands, eyeing me up. The three of them always tried to gang up on me. I felt their gazes sear my skin and ignored it. Years of putting up with their shit had thickened my skin.

Dante tipped the glass of scotch to his lips and laughed as he drank. "Nico is marrying the bride of Frankenstein." Another laugh. "Dad must hate you to make you marry that ugly bitch."

Angelo snorted with laughter. "More like the bride of Chucky."

Stefan snickered. "Nico does whatever Dad tells him to do. He's so desperate for his love."

"Fuck all of you," I shot back, anger surging through my veins. "If Dad told you to marry Vittoria, you would. So shut the fuck up!"

Dante leaned forward on the sofa, adjusting his cufflinks, his dark, menacing gaze meeting mine. "You better remember what I told you earlier. Don't get soft on us, Pretty Boy."

I hated that nickname.

At least I didn't have a nickname like Greasy Joe or Little Scarface. Some people whispered *re pazzo* behind Dante's back.

Mad king.

They would never say that shit to his face unless they had a death wish. I'd seen Dante whack people for less.

"I won't." I gritted my teeth. "The Vitales will wish they hadn't agreed to the marriage when I'm done with Vittoria."

Lies.

I didn't give a fuck about avenging the attack on Angelo. If I had to go through with the marriage, I would ignore Vittoria until she got bored with me. I had no intention of ever putting a hand on her. She was lucky she was engaged to me and not one of my brothers.

They would have killed her.

Dante raised his glass. "*Salute.*"

Chapter Two

AVA

Present Day

They were going to kill us. As I gasped for air, clutching my chest, each breath was more shallow than the last. I sat up straight, hoping it would help to clear my airway.

Nico hunched beside me and put his hand on my shoulder. "Ava, where's your inhaler?"

"Bathroom," I choked out, wheezing so badly my voice was hoarse.

"In the bathroom at your penthouse?" Nico clarified.

I bobbed my head.

Without another word, he ran out of the room and disappeared into the hallway.

"Can someone please get Ava a black coffee?" Dad asked with panic in his tone. "It will help to open her airway."

Salvatore snapped his fingers at the staff. "Coffee. Now!"

Seconds later, a woman slid a steaming cup of coffee in front of me. My hand shook as I lifted the mug and took a sip. Everyone stared at me like some circus freakshow.

My eyes shifted to Bella, who sat beside her parents. She had her hand over her heart, breathing almost as hard as me. This wasn't the first time she saw one of my attacks. The last time, she nearly fainted before she helped me find my inhaler that had fallen out of my purse.

Stefan put his hand on my thigh. "Ava, take slow breaths. Drink the coffee." Rubbing my knee, he softly said, "Just relax, okay?"

Why was he being so nice if they were going to kill me?

I nodded and drank from the cup, feeling some of the effects of the caffeine working through my body.

I liked Stefan.

He was funny and easygoing, the joker of the group. Whenever I was around him, I felt at ease. I could be myself and lower my guard. He even helped me work through my therapy techniques with me.

Angelo moved behind me and stroked my back in a circular motion, which helped to ease the tension. Stress worsened my asthma. I'd never been in a life or death type of situation until now.

"Deep breaths," he said in a soft tone.

I loved being cared for by the twins.

Of course, Dante didn't budge from his chair. He sat beside his father, staring at me from beneath his dark brows. A hint of concern touched his eyes, but his expression was unreadable.

Nico entered the dining room, shoved Angelo out of the way, and put the inhaler in front of my lips. "Here, baby," he whispered, tucking my hair behind my ear. "Take a deep breath."

After seeing me do it a few times, Nico knew what to do. I opened my mouth and took a slow, deep breath as he pressed down on the top of the canister. I held in the medicine for ten seconds and then blew it out before taking one more puff.

Everyone watched this odd display of affection from all three brothers. They gave me strange looks. If I were watching this play out, I would have wondered why these men were hovering around one woman.

To an outsider, it had to be obvious I was fucking all of them. The Lucianos wouldn't have done this for another employee.

Stefan was on my right, touching my leg like a protective

boyfriend. Angelo brushed his fingers beneath the strap of my dress over my bare skin. It seemed strange to have both of them fuss over me when I was seconds from death.

Or was I?

Maybe I had jumped to conclusions and made a scene for nothing.

Nico grazed my cheek with his knuckles. "Do you need me to call the doctor?"

I shook my head. "No, I don't think so."

He took my hands in his and sighed. "You have to remember to bring your inhaler with you." His gaze dropped to our hands. "Fuck, you can't scare me like that." He rubbed over the red marks on my wrist, and his jaw clenched as our eyes met. "Who did this to you?"

"Your brothers," I whispered.

His thumb traced over my skin as he looked at Angelo and Stefan. "I shouldn't have left you with them," he said in a hushed tone. "I'm sorry."

"I'm fine," I assured him since this wasn't the place to talk about the rough sex I had with the twins. So I clutched his hand and smiled. "Thank you, Nico. I'll be okay."

Stefan inched his hand up my thigh, snapping my attention back to him. "Are you feeling any better?"

I put my hand over his to stop him from going any farther. It didn't seem like he was going to pull an Angelo and try to finger me again at the dinner table. But as a precaution, I held his hand in place.

"I need some air," I muttered.

Angelo slid my chair out from the table. I rose to my feet with Stefan's help, and my kinky boss winked as our eyes met. He was becoming my new obsession. Something more than attraction drew me to Angelo. I couldn't quite put my finger on it, but I felt an odd sense of peace with him.

The Vitales looked down-right pissed. Their eyes flicked between Nico and me. They didn't seem to care as much about the twins touching me as they did Nico.

I was probably paranoid.

"I'll take her," Stefan offered.

Angelo touched my shoulder. "Feel better, *dolcezza.*"

Sweetness.

I loved their cute nicknames for me. If only Dante would stop being such an uptight dick and stop calling me Miss Vianello. It wouldn't have killed him to use my first name.

Angelo resumed his place at the table.

I glanced up at Nico, who towered over me, his big body invading my space. "You don't have to worry about me."

"I will always worry about you," he whispered.

After last night, there was no doubt in my mind that Nico had feelings for me. And I had them for him.

Stefan hooked his arm through mine. "Let's get you some air." He glanced at his father. "We won't be long, Papa."

I was hoping I could go outside with my dad, so we could talk. But Stefan insisted on accompanying me. Nico stayed behind and sat beside his father, who shot dagger eyes at him.

Stefan led me to the outdoor patio that overlooked the Atlantic Ocean. I had a similar view from my apartment. But Salvatore's patio was three times the size, had an even larger pool and spa, and a perfect view of the ocean.

Stefan steered me over to the table and sat beside me. "Are you sure you don't want me to call the doctor? I can get him over here in ten minutes."

When Stefan acted this way, I felt like he was my boyfriend. Not my boss or my captor. Not the man who would probably end up putting a bullet into my skull.

I shook my head, even though my chest was tight. "It will pass. The medicine is working."

He leaned forward and grabbed my hands, massaging my skin. "What triggered the asthma attack?"

"I don't know," I lied.

"No one was smoking. Was it someone's cologne? I know Paulie wears way too much." He tipped his head back and laughed. "And your friend Bella bathes in Chanel."

"No, it wasn't anything I smelled."

"You can talk to me, ya know." He tightened his grip on my fingers. "I'm not like Dante. I won't bite off your head."

"Thank you, Stefan, but I'm fine. I don't know what triggered it. Sometimes, it's out of my control."

"Is the salty air helping at all?"

"Yeah, a little bit." I let my hands fall away from his, so I could sit up straight and take slow breaths. "You should go back and eat dinner. I don't want to keep you."

"My dad has a rule. If one person is missing, none of us eat."

"Great." I sighed. "So we're holding everyone up?"

"Don't worry about it. Take all the time you need. The Vitales don't look like they've ever missed a meal. It won't kill them."

I shook my head and laughed. "Why are they here? I thought your family hated them?"

He scratched the corner of his jaw, deep in thought. "We're merging with them. Settling our old beef."

"Why?"

Stefan turned his head away from me, avoiding my gaze as he stared at the ocean. "My dad is getting closer to retirement, and he doesn't want us tearing apart the city anymore."

I let out a relieved breath.

And here, I thought they were all here because the Lucianos found out about the loan my dad got from the Vitales. So maybe they didn't have proof of my dad's crimes.

Sure, they had suspicions.

But so far, they couldn't prove anything. Even the forensic accountant digging through our files didn't spot anything out of the ordinary.

Stefan slid his chair closer to mine and hiked my dress up my thighs. Licking his lips, he ran his hands over my skin and hissed. "You're perfect, *bellezza*."

I liked when he called me beauty.

He dipped his head down and buried his face between my thighs, kissing up to my core. Each carefully placed kiss sent a shiver down my legs.

Fisting his black hair between my fingers, I closed my eyes and tilted my head back to rest it on the chair. "Stefan, they're waiting for us to eat dinner."

"They can wait five more minutes," he said against my skin.

I looked at the French doors, where a soft golden glow lit up the kitchen. "Can they see us out here?"

"They're not leaving the dining room." He pressed his index finger to his lips. "Be quiet and let me eat my dessert."

He pushed my panties to the side and licked me straight down the center, splitting me open with his tongue.

"Oh, God," I whispered, shoving my fingers through his hair. "Stefan."

His eyes met mine as he rolled his tongue over my aching clit and sucked it into his mouth. Much like his twin, Stefan enjoyed seeing the effect he had on me.

I moaned his name.

"That's it, sweet girl." He flicked his tongue. "Come for me."

Tremors of pleasure swept over my body like a violent storm. My legs trembled, and Stefan clutched my thighs, holding me in place as I came on his tongue.

"That wasn't smart," I said as he lifted his head.

He wiped his lips with the back of his hand. "Why not?"

"Because I just had an asthma attack," I muttered. "And I could hardly catch my breath when I came."

Stefan placed his arms on each side of the chair and kissed me. "I won't let anything happen to you."

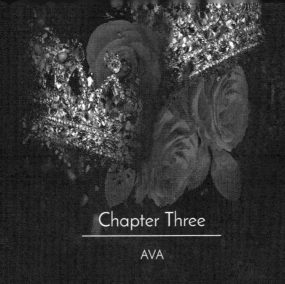

Chapter Three

AVA

As we entered the dining room, all conversation ceased. Everyone stared like I had something on my face. It made me feel even more insecure about what I had just done with Stefan. Like somehow, they knew what we did on the patio.

Stefan pulled out the chair for me and took his place beside me.

"Everything okay, Ava?" Salvatore asked, his voice deep and smooth.

I slapped on a fake smile. "Yes, Mr. Luciano. Sorry for delaying dinner."

"It's no trouble at all. Your health is our top priority."

His words put me at ease, and now I realized how much I had overreacted in the first place. But if we weren't here because of my dad, why did Salvatore invite so many people to dinner?

I hadn't spoken a single word to my dad. He looked so damn nervous, his hand shaking like crazy. He continued to down the contents of his glass, keeping his gaze on the table.

I lowered my head. "Thank you, Mr. Luciano. I appreciate your concern."

My dad raised me to be respectful to my bosses. He had instilled from a young age that the Lucianos were in power. And that it was our purpose in life to serve them.

They weren't going to kill us tonight, but they would find out the truth one day. Maybe by then, his sons would feel the same way about me as I did them. I wanted to help my dad but also felt guilty about it.

I didn't want to hurt them.

A moment later, the servers set antipasto trays on the table. Now that I could relax, I wanted to eat. So I plucked a piece of mozzarella and prosciutto from the plate and stuffed it into my mouth.

Vittoria Vitale was older than me, probably closer to thirty, and had frizzy black hair. As I ate my food, I noticed her eyes drift to Nico. She licked her lips as she undressed him.

Not like I could blame her.

But despite her constant staring, Nico ignored her.

The staff removed our empty plates to make room for Primi. They put dishes of the most delicious-smelling creamy gorgonzola gnocchi with spinach and pine nuts on the table.

I spooned the gnocchi onto my plate and stuffed it into my mouth, moaning when it hit my tongue.

Holy shit, it was incredible.

Stefan tapped my arm with his elbow. "Baby, when you make those sounds, I want to do dirty things to you." His lips brushed my earlobe, and I shivered from his touch. "Wait until later. I'm going to devour you."

I smiled and went back to eating.

Right before they served Secondi— Cotoletta alla Bolognese —Stefan put his hand on my leg and tapped his long fingers. He stared at me like I was his meal.

I dug my teeth into my lip.

Nico leaned over Stefan and whispered, "What did I tell you about biting that lip?"

I smiled so wide my cheeks hurt.

Our brief moment only lasted a few seconds before they served the next course. Something was off in Nico's body language. I felt his unease when he looked across the table at the Vitales.

Vincenzo Vitale spoke with Salvatore and Dante, mainly in Italian. For the most part, it sounded peaceful. But I could tell they had a strained relationship.

"I'm sorry," Nico whispered.

"For what?"

Nico snapped his head back to his dad when he called his name. They spoke about the casino and its expansion plans. Vincenzo chimed in with his ideas for a better version of Atlantic City.

After years of bloodshed, I wondered why they finally decided to settle their issues. I never thought I'd see the Lucianos and the Vitales in the same room, let alone share a meal.

By the time they served Contorni—Fagiolini all'agro—I was full and didn't feel like eating the green beans with lemon juice and olive oil.

But I didn't want to be rude.

Might as well eat like a king.

Before dessert, Salvatore stood at the end of the table and raised a champagne flute. "Thank you for coming to celebrate the union between two powerful families. After years of discourse, the Lucianos and the Vitales are coming together to make Atlantic City the city we all deserve."

He held out his glass, suggesting we do the same. And when our glasses were in position, he said, "To Nico and Vittoria. *Congratulazioni per il tuo fidanzamento.* May you have many happy years together." His gaze shifted to Nico, who looked like he wanted to hide under the table. "*Salute.*"

My jaw dropped at his words.

Congratulations on your engagement.

What.

The.

Fuck.

He lied to me.

It didn't matter what I thought anymore because it was a lie. I wanted so badly to believe Nico was better than his brothers and that he was more like me than them.

But I was wrong about him.

My hand wouldn't stop shaking, and the champagne flute slipped from my grasp. It hit the table, spilling champagne on the table cloth, my dress, and Stefan's pants.

Fuck.

Stefan shot up from the chair. The staff came over to assist him with the mess. And then, Stefan bent over me and dabbed at the champagne pooling on my lap.

I was too stunned to move.

Stefan waved his hand in front of my face. "Ava, look at me."

No.

Leave me alone.

I didn't want to do anything other than scream or cry. They all knew about Nico's engagement. The twins had sex with me knowing this, and so did Nico. I was so stupid to believe I could have anything more than sex with them.

My heart beat so fast that the entire room spun and slipped from under me. Nico was out of his chair, leaning over me. Stefan was at my side, talking to me, but I could only hear the ringing in my ears. His lips moved, but I didn't understand a word.

The people on the other side of the table blurred as if they were melting into the wall.

Nico was engaged.

Are you fucking kidding me?

I blinked. Once, twice, and a few more times, unable to clear my vision. The ringing in my ears made my head spin.

I wanted to cry.

I wanted to scream.

I wanted to kill him.

All five of the Vitales shot dagger eyes at me, annoyed with another interruption. I wasn't winning the favor of any of the Mafia families tonight.

Salvatore sat at the head of the table, the champagne flute in his hand. He hadn't gotten to finish his toast before I lost my

18

shit. If he didn't want to kill me before dinner, he probably did now.

"I'm so sorry, Mr. Luciano," I said to the Don. "I'm so clumsy."

"Take a minute to gather yourself, Ava." He snapped his fingers at the staff. "*Dolce.*"

I let out a sigh of relief.

The kitchen staff set the dessert dishes on the table. Then, the guests returned to talking amongst themselves as they layered their plates with sweet treats.

Dante didn't make a move for the food. His golden-brown eyes narrowed into slits, his anger radiating off him in waves.

He hated me.

No surprise there.

Bossman gritted his teeth and curled his hand into a fist on the table as his eyes stripped me bare. Angelo gave me a sympathetic look.

Did he feel sorry for me?

I felt so fucking pathetic.

Nico leaned over Stefan to speak to me. "It's not what you think," he said in a hushed tone. "*Mi dispiace, passerotta.* Just let me explain."

I gripped the knife in front of me, teeth clenched. "Don't call me that. I never want to speak to you again."

"Ava, please," he whispered. "I know what you're thinking—"

"No, you don't," I fired back, fighting the tears threatening to spill down my cheeks. "You have no idea what this feels like." I shook my head and lowered my voice. "*Sono un idiota.*"

Nico sighed. "You're not an idiot."

Mr. Vitale glared at Nico, then aimed his hateful gaze at me. His wife pursed her lips, sitting beside Vittoria, who tipped up her nose at us. Carlo and Joey watched each of us with equal intensity. They knew something was going on with Nico and me.

I didn't want to be on the shit list of a powerful Mafia family. It was bad enough I had to launder money for the Lucianos. God only knew what would happen to me if one of the Vitales decided I was a problem.

Or worse?

What if they told the Lucianos about my father's loan? If the families were merging, wouldn't they eventually have to share their outstanding debts? I wasn't sure what this marriage entailed or how the merger worked.

Nico leaned over Stefan's arm. "Give me five minutes to explain."

I shook my head. "No, we're done."

Before I could stab him with the knife, Stefan gripped my wrist. "If you want to kill Pretty Boy, I'll help you. But not here, okay?"

My entire body trembled, making it harder to maintain my grip on the knife.

Stefan took it from me, dropped it onto the table with a clang, and slid his arm behind my back.

I blew out a deep breath. "Did you know?"

He looked away.

They knew Nico was engaged to Vittoria Vitale and let me make an ass of myself.

"Hey, baby," he whispered. "I know you're mad. But it's going to be okay."

"Don't call me your baby," I muttered. "All of you are liars."

Stefan helped me up from the chair. "Let's go. I'll tell you everything."

We left the room without asking to be excused by Salvatore. I doubted he cared after all the drama I brought to his dinner table.

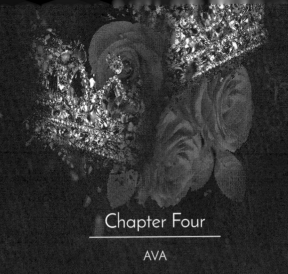

Chapter Four

AVA

S tefan guided me out of Salvatore's penthouse and into mine. Once inside the living room, Stefan hooked his arm around me and pulled me onto the couch beside him.

"Look, we didn't know until this morning about the engagement. My dad mentioned it a few weeks ago as a possibility. The Vitales have been our rivals for a long time. So we didn't think it would ever happen."

I shrugged his hand off my shoulder and scooted across the leather cushion. "Did you know Nico was engaged when you took me to La Perla?"

He nodded.

"Did Nico know when we were together this morning?"

"He got the phone call from our dad after he woke up."

My cheeks heated from his confession, every inch of my skin on fire from the betrayal. "Nico didn't think twice about fucking me again." I blew out a deep breath, nostrils flaring. "What an asshole."

My eyes drifted to the patio doors. I wanted to scream until my throat was raw. So I hopped up from the couch and walked toward the kitchen.

"Where do you think you're going?" Stefan snapped his fingers. "Get back here, Ava."

I strolled out of the living room. "No."

"We're not done talking." Stefan followed me. "Stop acting like a brat."

I pushed open the doors and stepped outside, drinking in the salty air. We stood in front of the railing. Stefan was aware of my process and let me have a moment. So he held my hand and screamed with me, which comforted me.

It wasn't like he was the one who was engaged. Though, I wished he had told me the truth earlier. He could have tipped me off so I hadn't made a fool of myself.

After we yelled a few more times, I glanced at Stefan, who was already looking at me. "You said you wanna talk. So talk."

He snorted at my bitchiness. "You're lucky I'm not Dante. He would've spanked your ass until it was raw."

I put my hand over the top of his on the railing. "I know it's fucked up to expect Nico to be loyal to me when I fucked you and Angelo earlier."

This was something I had been thinking about a lot lately. How could I expect them to be faithful to me? As Dante had pointed out, I was jumping between his brothers. I didn't feel like a whore or think it made me one.

"I like all of you." I bit the inside of my cheek as our eyes met. "I know I shouldn't. It's sick, right?"

He gave a light shrug, making his broad shoulders look even bigger. "What's sick about it?"

"The four of you are brothers."

He snorted. "Oh, now you're including Dante in our little fucked up sex group?"

"I mean…" I bit my lip, thinking over his question. "He jerked off on my stomach while I fingered myself. That counts, I guess."

"I don't know about all that. Dante is not your biggest fan. That's for fucking sure."

"He said I was supposed to be different."

I leaned into his muscular body for support, needing to feel him pressed against me.

"When Dante choked me with his belt, he listed all the reasons I disappointed him." I shifted my stance so that I could look up at him. He was at least ten inches taller than me. "What does he want from me? No matter how hard I try to please your brother, he still hates me."

"Dante is old school." Stefan stared at the Atlantic Ocean as the waves crashed on the beach. "He raised Angelo and me. We were eleven when our mom died. So Dante stepped up and took over for our dad."

"That must have been hard for all of you."

He nodded. "My brother carries the weight of our entire family on his shoulders. He's been doing it since he was your age. It's how he's wired. So don't take it personally."

I almost laughed at his suggestion. Everything Dante said and did to me felt personal. Like he lived to make my life miserable. He enjoyed pushing me out of my comfort zone.

"Dante hates me for no reason." I released a deep sigh. "I haven't done anything wrong."

Stefan leaned forward, using the railing to support himself. "Dante will never tell you this, but he wants a woman like our mom."

That wasn't what I expected.

"What was your mom like?"

"She was a fucking saint. The perfect Mafia wife." Stefan inched closer until our elbows touched. "Dante was in the car with my parents the night our mom died. A bullet meant for my dad. Two inches to the left, and it would have killed Dante."

I gasped at his confession.

"Dante was sitting right next to her." He scrubbed a hand across his jaw and groaned. "He had her blood on his face, his clothes, even in his mouth. I remember him coming home from the hospital, still covered in her blood hours later. It was like he didn't want to wash it off his skin. Like he thought it would make her death permanent. I don't think he could process she was gone."

"I can't imagine what that must have been like for him."

"Me neither." He shoved a hand through his black hair to push it off his forehead. "Angelo and I didn't know our mom the way Dante did. And we didn't have to see her die in front of us. That kind of trauma sticks with you."

I nodded. "My mom hasn't been in my life since high school. She was causing too much trouble for my dad, so he sent her away. But I can't even fathom seeing her die."

"Give Dante a break." He stepped back from the railing. "That's all I'm sayin'. He's not a bad guy. Just a little fucked up. But aren't all of us a little screwed up in our own way?"

"I'm not perfect. Look at what I've been doing with you and your brothers for the past few weeks."

"Liking sex doesn't make you bad." He slid his fingers beneath my chin. "You were sheltered for most of your life. And now you're living. Nothing wrong with that."

"How are you so calm all the time? Nothing seems to bother you."

"Someone's gotta lighten the mood around here." He laughed. "Angelo is a fucking mad man. Dante is so worried about losing his cool that he forgets to take the stick out of his ass. And Nico... He's not bad. Just not my favorite person."

"Because he's your dad's bastard?"

He shook his head. "Nah, that's Dante's issue with him. Nico tries too hard to make everyone like him. It fucking annoys Angelo and me."

"I liked Nico from the start." My chest ached as I thought about Nico and my blossoming feelings for him. "He makes it so easy."

Stefan snickered. "I think you liked his pretty-boy face and big dick more than his personality." He tapped me with his elbow. "Admit it. He's too much of a people pleaser."

"So am I."

Why was it so easy to lower my guard with Stefan? I often felt my walls come crumbling down around him.

He was a good listener.

I liked that about him.

24

Stefan clutched my hip. "You're still a good girl. Fucking three brothers won't send you straight to Hell."

I looked up at him and smiled. "I don't want to be the girl I used to be. But somewhere in the middle sounds good."

"Stick around here long enough, and you'll have to choose one path."

"I made my choice when I agreed to work for you."

"Not like you had a choice." He snickered. "My dad offered you a job you literally couldn't refuse."

"Until my graduation, I never had a real family." Pressing my palm to his chest, I felt the steady beat of his heart. "The night Dante made us dinner reminded me of what I wanted as a kid and never got. I like being part of your family."

"You're not going anywhere." He moved me in front of him, so we could look at the ocean. "We're keeping you, Ava. And there ain't a damn thing you can do about it."

"Good." My cheeks hurt from smiling. "Because I want you to keep me."

Stefan kissed the top of my head. "Feeling better, *bellezza*?"

I shrugged. "I still don't understand why Nico has to marry Vittoria."

"Paulie, my dad's advisor, came up with the idea. He suggested it to my dad as a way to broker peace with the Vitales. So the old man met with Vincenzo Vitale since he hasn't found anyone who will marry Vittoria."

"I can't imagine why," I said with laughter in my tone.

Stefan chuckled. "Better Nico than me. I'd jump off this building if I had to marry that uptight bitch."

"Is she that bad?"

"We hate the Vitales." His grip tightened around me. "Ever since Carlo fucked up Angelo's face, we've been planning how to get rid of them. Then my dad suggested Nico marry Vittoria and threw all of us through a loop."

"Why did he wait until this morning to tell Nico?"

"Our dad likes to spring shit on us last minute. Nico is only doing this to avoid another war with the Vitales. It has nothing

25

to do with you. If it were up to Nico, he'd be here right now with you." He cupped the side of my face, and I leaned into his hand. "It makes sense. This is how we do things in our world. We marry for power."

"Would you have married Vittoria if your dad asked you?"

Stefan rested his chin on my head and held me. "Just like you, we can't refuse the boss. Everyone's gotta take orders from someone."

"I want to go home for the night." Tilting my head back on his chest, I looked at him. "Do you think that would be allowed? Or am I a prisoner here?"

He considered my question and then dropped his hands from my body. "You wanna go home?"

I spun around to look at him. "Just for the night. I want to see Angelina and Enzo and get a break from Nico and this engagement shit." I swiped at the single tear that slid down my cheek. "Please, Stefan. I'll come back tomorrow."

Stefan reached into his pocket and removed his cell phone, fingers flying across the keypad. "I'll drive you. But don't mention this to Dante, okay?"

"Who are you texting?"

"Angelo," he said as we walked into the house. "I told him to keep Dante busy until I get back." He stuffed the phone into his pocket and grabbed my hand, leading me toward the front door. "I'll pick you up in the morning. Don't try anything stupid."

"I won't," I promised.

Chapter Five

AVA

All the way home, the tears would not stop falling. I hated crying in front of Stefan, but Nico broke me. I'd never had a real relationship. So the Luciano brothers were technically my longest relationship to date.

Stefan let me cry and vent on the ten-minute ride to my house. I lived in a brick colonial on the edge of Atlantic City. It had a big yard with a perfectly manicured lawn and trimmed hedges lining the property—the typical cookie-cutter suburban home.

Stefan parked in the circular driveway and tapped his fingers on the leather steering wheel. "Do you want me to walk you inside?"

I pushed open the door and shook my head. "No, that's okay."

He reached across the car and clutched my hip. "Where do you think you're going without kissing me goodbye?"

My insides melted at his words. Stefan was by no means soft, but I liked this side of him. He wasn't a big, scary Mafia man with me.

So I turned my head and parted his lips with my tongue. He palmed the back of my head, deepening the kiss as he tugged at my dress like he wanted to rip it off me. We kissed for what felt like hours before our lips separated. And when he looked into my eyes, breathless, I knew there was something special brewing between us.

"Thanks, Stefan." I placed a soft peck on his lips. "I won't forget this."

"I'll be here tomorrow at nine on the dot." He tapped his fingers on the steering wheel. "If I have to come in there and get you, I'm dragging your pretty ass out by your hair."

"Yes, sir."

Stefan snorted. "This fucking girl," he muttered as if he were talking more to himself than to me.

I got out of the car and hurried into the house.

One night of freedom.

Free from them.

And the obligation.

Pretty soon, my dad would be home, and then we could talk about handling his shady business with the Vitales. I needed to know more about the loan, like how much he owed them. We hadn't talked about more than work since the day out front of Starbucks when he confessed his crimes. Our employers watched us every second.

So this was our only chance.

And now that our lives were safe for the night, I could relax and formulate a coherent plan. I needed the time and space from the Luciano brothers to gather my thoughts.

I waved to Stefan before I walked inside the house. He returned the gesture and then peeled out from the driveway. The tires screeched as he sped away in the black Ferrari.

On my way to the kitchen, I ran into Angelina. She was an older woman with graying hair who had raised me. My nanny. But she was more like a mother to me.

"What's wrong, *bambina*?"

I didn't bother to hide the tears or wipe them away. "Nico Luciano is marrying Vittoria Vitale."

"Why are you so upset?" Angelina pulled me into her arms and hugged me, stroking her fingers down my back.

"Because we were together. I mean... I don't know what we were doing. But I liked him. I was so stupid to think we could have a relationship."

"So that's why the Don summoned your father to his penthouse? To announce Nico's engagement?"

I nodded, taking a step back to compose myself. "Nico could have told me." I dropped my purse on the kitchen island and sat on a stool. "I made a fool of myself. Spilled champagne on the table, my dress, and Stefan's pants." I shook my head, hair falling in front of my eyes. "It was so embarrassing."

"How did you get home?" Angelina opened the freezer and removed a carton of chocolate ice cream. "Where is your father?"

"He's still at the Portofino. Stefan drove me home."

She put the ice cream on the counter and grabbed a can of whipped cream, maraschino cherries, chocolate syrup, and sprinkles. Whenever I felt like shit, Angelina knew how to cheer me up. Even before Dad sent my mom away, she wasn't around much. My mother was usually busy drinking away her feelings over my dad's work. It killed her that she married the Mafia.

After my mom discovered the truth, she started drinking and popping pills, living in a drug-induced state to numb the pain. She was in California in another rehab. But she called it a wellness clinic.

At least she wasn't here.

Maybe she would have a chance to avoid the fallout. I could see the tension between my dad and Salvatore at dinner. We were only biding our time until the Lucianos did something about his betrayal.

Enzo walked into the kitchen as Angelina made me an ice cream sundae. He was Angelina's husband and had been my family's chef since I was a child.

Enzo came up beside me and placed his hand on my shoulder. "I thought I heard you crying, *stellina*."

Little star.

I smiled at his nickname for me.

When I was a kid, he said I had a bright future. That I was

29

even more talented than my father and would become a star so bright I would light up the entire solar system. He was a better father to me than my dad.

"I'm okay," I told him. "Just upset about dinner."

"Nico Luciano is marrying Vittoria Vitale," Angelina said, one eyebrow raised.

Enzo glanced down at me, saw the tears, then his gaze was back on Angelina. "Oh." He sat on the stool beside me and rubbed his hand down my back. "You're a sweet girl, Ava. Nico would have swallowed you whole and spit you out. Men like that don't keep women around for long. Even his wife won't be the only woman in his life." His long fingers brushed through my hair. "They might be the boardwalk kings, but eventually, the Lucianos will end up behind bars."

I sniffed back the tears and nodded. "I'm an idiot."

"No, you're not." He gave me a one-arm hug. "You're a smart girl. It's easy to overlook things with the Lucianos. Your father has done it for a long time."

I heard the front door slam. Dad walked into the kitchen, tugging at his tie. He looked like he had aged twenty years in the past few weeks. The stress of his sins weighed down on him.

My dad threw his keys onto the kitchen island, his jaw clenched. "Everyone out! I need to speak with my daughter. Alone."

Angelina and Enzo left the room without a word.

"Dad, I know what you're going to say—"

He pushed out his palm to silence me. "We don't need the Vitales as enemies. I have enough shit to deal with right now."

"I'm sorry," I muttered. "It just happened with Nico. I didn't mean to get caught up with him."

"Excuses." He rounded the island so we had some distance between us, his intimidating glare slicing through me. "Nicodemus is a made man. A captain. Do you have any idea what kind of enemies they have? Not to mention that you exposed your relationship in front of his fiancee."

"I didn't know Nico was engaged to Vittoria. He never mentioned it."

He shook his head, scrubbing a hand across the dark stubble on his jaw. "And why would Nico mention his fiancee to his *puttana*?"

"Don't call me that!" I slid off the chair and approached him. "How dare you? I'm not a whore."

"Did you think you would be anything else to a man like Nico? You are my daughter, and I will not let you ruin your life." He opened the freezer, grabbed a vodka bottle, and drank from it. "I'm sending you away before they kill you."

"No," I fired back. "I'm staying here with Angelina and Enzo for the night."

"I know you think of them as your parents, but I hate to break it to you, Ava. They are the staff."

"I hate you." My top lip quivered as I spoke. "You're mad they were better parents than you and Mom."

"Hate me all you want." He downed half the bottle in one gulp. "It doesn't change the fact I'm right." He leaned his back against the counter, bottle clutched in his hand. "Salvatore didn't invite us to his house to celebrate the engagement."

"Then, why?"

"To see how we would act around him." He pushed off the counter and put the almost empty bottle on the island. "He's getting closer to uncovering my lies. I can feel it."

"What's going to happen to you?"

"I dug my grave." He sighed. "You know how to access their accounts, right?"

I nodded to confirm.

"If anything happens to me, I want you to move all of it offshore. Use it as leverage to stay alive. Don't let the Lucianos have power over you. Because once they get the money, they will kill you."

"Dad, what am I supposed to do?"

"There's an offshore account for you." He ran his fingers through his hair to push it off his forehead. "You'll need a key to access the money. It's in my safe. There are fake credentials and enough money for you to live on for a while. If this ends the way I think it will, I want you to buy a one-way plane ticket to the Bahamas."

I swallowed hard to clear the lump forming at the back of my throat. It felt like someone was stabbing me in the gut, taking a blade to my insides. "Dad, you're scaring me."

"I'm sorry. I made a choice a long time ago. I thought I could walk away whenever I wanted."

My top lip trembled. "I'm scared."

He wrapped his arm around me and kissed my head like a real father who cared about his daughter. "You'll get through this. So will your mother. She's safe in California."

"What will happen to you?"

"Don't worry about me. I have a plan."

Chapter Six

NICO

After dinner, Dad walked Vincenzo Vitale to the front door with his hand on his back. I never thought I'd see the two bosses coming together. And it was at the cost of my relationship with Ava.

She hated me.

Stefan had disappeared while we ate dessert and didn't return until after we finished eating. He looked like he was up to something. Even Dante noticed and asked him what happened to Ava. He waved his hand and said to leave her alone for the night.

Giancarlo left my father's penthouse the second the staff removed the plates from the table. As usual, he drank too much and shook uncontrollably. It was so obvious he was hiding something from us. Every time he had to speak to my father, he looked uncomfortable.

I wondered if his behavior made Ava so on edge that it triggered her asthma attack. Or maybe it was Paulie's foul-smelling cologne.

Dad patted Vincenzo on the back. "We'll speak soon about the engagement party."

Vittoria hooked her arm through mine and pulled me aside. She glanced up at me with those dark brown eyes that appeared black. Even her clothes didn't have an ounce of color. I couldn't believe I had to marry this woman when I had Ava in the apartment beside mine.

Ava was a natural beauty.

And so perfect for me.

Vittoria dug her long nails into my arm and lowered her voice to a menacing tone. "Is that girl going to be a problem for us?"

Fuck.

"No," I lied. "She's nothing to me."

She gritted her teeth. "Didn't seem like nothing."

I shrugged. "What do you want me to say? Ava Vianello is young and has a crush on me."

Vittoria flicked her long, dark hair over her shoulder and snickered. Then she stared at the diamond engagement ring on her finger with a smile. If I were going to propose to a woman, it would have been with the massive rock my dad gave my mother. A promise of his love, even though he couldn't marry her.

The past was repeating itself with Ava and me. We would never marry, but we could still be together. My parents had made it work for the past thirty years.

"I think it's safe to say neither of us wants this," Vittoria tossed back with an attitude. "If I find out anything is going on with the two of you, I won't think twice about ending the engagement."

"You have nothing to worry about," I assured her.

She flashed a closed-mouth smile and left the penthouse with her mom. Carlo and Angelo glared at each other. The joining of our families wouldn't settle the feud. Every time Angelo looked in the mirror, he remembered Carlo.

That scar haunted him.

Dante spoke to Joey in a strained tone, like it was painful for him to utter a single word to him. He was seconds from wringing his fucking neck. When Carlo attacked Angelo, he took it personally. Like the scar left on Angelo's cheek was on his skin.

Stefan stood beside Angelo, glaring at Carlo. They both looked ready to put a bullet in his skull.

After the Vitales left, Mom floated into the living room like she was walking on air. She was a dancer, so graceful on her feet. Whenever she entered a room, people noticed her.

My mom sat beside me and stroked my cheek with her fingers, same as when I was a kid. "I know this isn't what you wanted. But it will all work out."

"Thanks, Ma." I kissed her cheek. "We have to talk to Dad." I tipped my head at my brothers, who gathered on the couch around my father. "You should go back to your apartment. I'll stop by later."

My mother glanced at my brothers. They were giving her their usual annoyed looks. It didn't matter how many years passed because they still hated her.

"Okay," she whispered. "I'll see you later."

She moved behind my father in the armchair and whispered into his ear. I watched as his usual stern expression slipped for a split second, the corner of his mouthing pulling up into a smile. He tapped his fingers on her hand and nodded.

After she was gone, my dad got up from the chair and walked over to me. He bent down and whacked me on the side of the head. "*Idiota.* I told you to get closer to the girl. Not fuck her! Look at the scene the two of you made at my dinner table. The Vitales are not stupid."

My dad always had the power to reduce all of us to children. He often smacked the twins and me. Dante never stepped out of line—the perfect Mafia boss in training.

I rubbed the side of my head. "I'm sorry. I didn't think Ava would react that way. It's not like I had the chance to tell her about the engagement. She was with Stefan all day."

He stepped back, his eyes moving between us. "What is happening with the four of you and that girl?"

"Nothing," Dante shot back. "I'm still on board to kill her."

"I'm not," Angelo interjected.

"Then reattach your fucking balls," Dante hissed. "All three of you are pussy whipped."

Angelo snickered. "Fuck you. No, I'm not."

"Giancarlo was acting stranger than usual." Dante's eyes shifted to my father. "The guilt is killing him. Eventually, he will confess to his daughter. And then, we'll get rid of that family of thieves."

"Ava isn't the one stealing from us," I reminded him.

"We don't know that," Dante fired back.

"I do," I said with certainty. "She's not helping her dad. Trust me. I know Ava better than all of you."

"Now that you're out of play," my dad said to me, "it puts us in a precarious situation."

"She likes Angelo and me," Stefan said. "We can get through to her."

Dante snarled. "You can't fuck her into a confession."

Angelo shook his head and laughed. "We'll see about that."

"I have a better idea." Dad dropped into the armchair across from us. "Dante, I want you to get closer to Ava."

His usual stony expression slipped. "She's not going to confide in me, Pop. I scare her."

"No, you don't," Angelo told him.

"She's dying for you to touch her," Stefan said. "We had a long talk about you earlier. Ava's got it bad for you."

Dante's eyes narrowed. "Why are we bothering with this shit? I say we round up the Vianellos and torture the information out of them."

"Giancarlo is one of my oldest friends." Dad lifted a glass from the table. "Until we have proof, I don't want to make accusations. I was the best man at his wedding. I'm Ava's godfather. It's my responsibility to protect her. You understand that."

Dante nodded. "Of course. So what do you want me to do?"

"Show Ava what you do at the hotel and casino. Make her feel more comfortable, part of the family."

"No offense, Papa," Angelo cut in, "but Dante's not exactly welcoming. He's more likely to kill her than get her talking."

Stefan chuckled. "I got money on Dante losing his shit after one day with her."

Dad pointed his finger at Stefan. "Shut your mouth, boy."

Stefan raised his hands in defense. "Sorry, Papa."

They called me a good boy.

A good dog.

But they were just as respectful to our father. Even when we talked back, and he put us in our places, we cowered to him. He was the boss of our family. We respected the shit out of him.

"It's settled." Dad rose from the armchair and drank from the glass in his hand. "Starting on Monday, Dante will work closely with Ava." Then he looked at the twins and me. "I want all of you to make her life easier. No more games or bullshit. I'll be with Cara until morning. Don't disappoint me."

He left the living room.

"I can't wait to see what happens with Dante and Ava." Angelo winked. "That girl is a firecracker. She'll push Dante so far out of his comfort zone that he snaps."

Dante shot up from the chair like it was on fire, his teeth clenched. "I'll get the information none of you pussies could."

He stormed out of the room, ending the conversation.

ater that night, I went down to my mother's apartment. I needed to talk to someone about Ava and this fucking engagement hanging over my head.

Ma always knew what to do and had an answer in complicated situations like this one, especially matters of the heart.

I stopped in front of her door and knocked. A few seconds later, she opened the door, dressed in a black lace teddy paired with thigh-highs and an attached garter belt.

"Jesus, Ma." I turned my head away from her. "Put some fucking clothes on."

She stepped to the side to allow me inside the apartment. "Is this how you greet your mother?"

I glanced down at her, with her tits falling out of the top, and shook my head. "Clothes, Ma. Please."

She groaned. "I dance in less than this." My mother grabbed a short silk robe from the couch. "Stop being such a prude, Nico."

"I'm not a prude. I don't want to see you naked."

Mom stood on her tippy toes to wrap her arms around my neck, and I hugged her back, lifting her feet off the floor. I kissed her cheek. "How are you doing, Ma?"

"You know me. I go with the flow." She gripped my biceps and looked up at me with the same light blue eyes she'd given me. "I'm more concerned with how you're doing."

I sat on the couch beside her and shrugged. "I was hoping Dad wouldn't make me go through with the engagement."

"Ava is important to you." So intuitive, she leaned into me, already reading the truth on my face. "You care for her."

I nodded. "But it's complicated. She's the daughter of Giancarlo Vianello. Ava was supposed to be a mark, someone for me to use and throw away."

"It doesn't have to be the end," she said softly. "Look at your father and me. He was married for more than half of our relationship."

"How do you do it with Dad?"

She sighed. "Baby, I knew your father was married. I didn't care. I fell hard for him and didn't give a damn about the consequences."

"But how did you deal with being separated from him all the time?"

She tucked her legs beneath her and pressed her red glossed lips together. "It wasn't easy. But I knew what I was getting myself into when I met Salvatore. I saw the wedding band on his finger. I was young and naive. He spoiled me rotten and treated me like a queen. When I was with him, nothing else mattered. It still doesn't. Even after thirty years as his mistress, I would do it again. I have no regrets."

I leaned back against the cushion. "You're more than his mistress."

A grin stretched the corners of her mouth, lighting up her eyes. "I know, baby. We don't need to marry for me to know I'm the love of your father's life. Great loves don't die. They thrive even in the darkness. If you care for Ava, you can find a way to make it work."

"She's not like you." I ran a hand through my hair and groaned. "Ava didn't go into this thinking she would have to share me with another woman."

"Vittoria will be your wife in name. Same as Giulia was to your father. In his heart and mind, he was mine."

"Giulia had the twins five years after he met you. Dad wasn't faithful to either of you."

"Men have needs." Mom kicked her long legs out in front of her, crossing her ankles on the coffee table. "He fucked her sometimes. I didn't care. We had an agreement. And after the twins were born, he didn't touch her again." She cradled the side of my face in her hand. "Your father loves you. But he needed more children with Giulia to expand his empire. He cared too much about his legacy."

"I know."

"You're his son. A Luciano. I'm so proud of you, Nico." She smiled. "Your father did a good job raising you."

"So did you." I held her hand on the couch. "I missed you."

I was almost thirty years old and still needed my mom. It sounded pathetic.

Whatever.

She was my rock and had been for my entire life. Whenever I couldn't deal with my brothers or the mistreatment at home, she always knew what to say.

"Where's Dad?"

She tipped her head toward the back of the apartment. "Sleeping. I wore him out."

"Ma," I groaned. "Please."

"You're old enough to know what I do with your father." She chuckled and got up from the couch, beckoning me with her finger. "Come, I ordered your favorite dessert from the bakery."

I sat on a stool in the kitchen as she removed a plate of chocolate chip cannoli from the refrigerator. "Something is off with Dad and this engagement. I can tell you're putting on a strong front for me. But I need advice."

She put two cannoli on a plate and slid them in front of me. "Your dad has been acting a little strange." Mom glanced over her shoulder, checking for my father. "I asked Salvatore what he wants to do for our anniversary, and he forgot the date."

I lifted the pastry and took a bite. "That's odd."

"I know." She sat in the chair beside me and lowered her voice. "I'm worried about him."

"Why didn't you say something sooner?"

"I didn't notice until last night when we were in bed." She reached across the island and grabbed a cannoli from the plate. "He sounded fine over the phone. But I haven't had much time to talk to him lately. I've been so busy with my dance crew."

I finished off the second pastry, speaking between bites. "Do you think there's something wrong with Dad?"

Mom shrugged. "I hope not." She put her hand on my knee. "Keep an eye on your father."

I bobbed my head. "Of course, Ma."

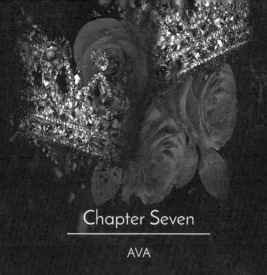

Chapter Seven

AVA

I woke up with a headache and blood soaking my shorts. So I got out of bed and stripped off the sheets, adding them to the laundry basket.

Yay for periods!

I went into the bathroom and cleaned up. Then I hopped into the shower and got ready for the day. Once I looked presentable, wearing a red Valentino dress and black pumps, I headed to the twins' apartment.

Stefan would take me to the store.

I knocked on the door, and after banging on it five times, I heard Angelo yell, "You better be fucking dying or have a death wish to be knocking on my door this early."

"Angelo, it's me."

The door flung open, and Angelo stood in the entryway in a pair of gray boxer briefs. His dick was hard and poked through the slit, showing off his piercing.

I checked out his muscular, tattooed chest and licked my lips. "Excited to see me?"

"Morning wood, baby." Angelo put his hand on my back and steered me into the apartment, slamming the door behind us. "But yeah, that, too." He gripped my ass. "You look good enough to eat." Then he kissed my neck and breathed in my perfume. "Why are you up so early, pretty girl?"

Before I could respond, Stefan entered the kitchen naked. He stood with the refrigerator door open, drinking orange juice from the bottle. "Miss us already?" Stefan asked between sips, raising his hand. "Come over here. I got someone who wants to say hello."

I laughed at his playfulness.

He was also hard and looked like he had just woken up. His short, dark hair stuck up in different places. But he still looked good all tatted up, his muscular body on display for me.

Stefan walked into the living room. And with the twins surrounding me, I couldn't catch my breath. Angelo hooked his arm around me from behind, so I could feel him on my back. Then Stefan pressed his chest to mine, and his dick rubbed my stomach.

"You guys are killing me," I whispered.

I used a wad of toilet paper as my temporary pad and needed to get to the store immediately. The first few days of my flow were heavy. So this makeshift setup would not last long.

Someone knocked on the door.

"What the fuck?" Angelo grunted, his hand falling from my body. "Why is everyone coming over so fucking early? Like we weren't up all night working." He opened the door. "What?"

"Don't you fucking what me," Dante snapped as he pushed past Angelo to enter the room. He glanced at me, and then his gaze shifted back to Angelo. "What is she doing here?"

I rolled my eyes at the prick. "Good morning to you, too."

Dante's nostrils flared as he shoved up his suit jacket sleeve to inspect his watch. "You have one hour until you start work."

I forced a smile. "I'll be there with bells on."

My response garnered a snarl from Dante.

Angelo slid his arm across the back of Dante's neck. He didn't look as disgusted as when I touched him, but it wasn't much better. "What do you need, boss?"

"Johnny Z is going to be a problem for us."

Stefan ran a hand through his messy black hair. "What now?"

Dante's jaw clenched as he looked at the twins. "Our guys heard a rumor. He's planning to poach our girls."

I assumed he was talking about the strippers and prostitutes at the clubs. Johnny Zabatino ran a small Mafia family on the other side of Atlantic City. He also owned strip clubs and bars.

"I'll handle him," Stefan said.

Angelo tapped Dante's shoulder. "We got it covered."

Stefan bent down to kiss my lips. "Morning, beauty."

I kissed him back, and when I glanced at Dante, he looked repulsed. "Why do you look so grossed out when I kiss your brothers?"

Dante crossed his arms over his suit-clad chest and rolled his eyes.

The twins laughed.

"Dante, kiss a woman?" Angelo howled with laughter. "That would be the fucking day."

"Why?" I asked. "What's the big deal?"

"I'm sure you've noticed Dante doesn't like to be touched." Angelo aimed a pointed look at his older brother. "He's never even kissed a woman."

My eyes widened. "Really?"

Dante glared at me. "Not like it's any of your business, but I don't need to kiss a woman to fuck them. It's not a prerequisite to sex."

"Actually," I bit out, "it is for most people."

"Not for big bro," Stefan added with a chuckle. "He won't even let the whores look at him when he fucks them."

"Shut up! If you know what's good for you, stop talking."

"Aww, Dante is butt hurt." Stefan snickered. "I guess we're all getting punished."

Dante stepped in front of him. "Stop fucking talking about my personal life in front of our employee."

"Ava is more than our employee. Dad is her godfather. And we take care of our family."

"What are you talking about?" I narrowed my eyes at him. "Your dad isn't my godfather."

"It's true," Dante confirmed.

"Why didn't I know that?"

Dante shrugged. "Ask your father. He's good at keeping secrets."

Fuck.

Was he telling me he knew about the money my father stole from them? And now that the Lucianos and Vitales were merging, would they have to share their outstanding debts? Would my father's crimes become more apparent?

I hope not.

"Anyway, I came over here because I need things…"

Dante fixed one of his hateful stares at me, stuffing his hands into his pockets. "What kind of things?"

If I were still on good terms with Nico, I would have asked him. But he was engaged, so that left Stefan.

"It's that time of the month."

Stefan ran his fingers through his messy hair, oblivious to the fact he was naked. Or maybe he didn't care. "What time?"

I blew out a deep breath and groaned. "Haven't you guys spent any time around women?"

Angelo snickered. "Not longer than it takes to fuck them."

They grunted in agreement.

"Oh, that time," Stefan said after an awkward pause. "She's saying she has her period. You guys are fucking dense."

"Ding, ding, ding." I raised my hand and smirked. "We have a winner."

"You need tampons or whatever?" Stefan asked.

I nodded. "Unless you want me to bleed all over this apartment."

Dante's nose wrinkled.

Stefan lifted his cell phone from the table, his fingers moving across the keypad. "Mrs. Destefano will hook you up."

"Who is Mrs. Destefano?"

He raised his hand to silence me as he spoke to the woman

44

on the other end. Then he handed the phone to me. She asked me what kind of feminine products I needed and said she would have them delivered to my apartment.

I handed the phone to Stefan. "Thank you."

Angelo snaked his arm around my middle, pressing his hard dick between my ass cheeks. "We can still play, baby."

"Do you not know how periods work?" I leaned back on his chest to look up at him. "I'm bleeding down there."

"I cut out a man's heart with a hunting knife." His hand inched up my chest and over my breast. "Now that's a lot of fucking blood."

I shook my head. "That's oddly descriptive and disturbing."

"I'm not afraid of a little blood." He licked my neck and shoved his hand between my thighs. "It won't stop me from fucking you." Angelo's nose brushed my cheek. "I'm getting even harder just thinking about your blood all over my dick."

"You're either perfect or insane." I smiled. "Still not sure which one."

"Insane," Stefan interjected. "Angelo hasn't been right since—"

Angelo's hand shot out to silence Stefan. "Don't fucking talk about that night."

"Calm down, killer." I spun around, put my palms on his chest, and stood on my tippy toes. "You don't have to bite our heads off whenever someone mentions your scar." I pressed my lips to his right cheek. "It doesn't make you ugly, Angelo. You're one of the sexiest men I've ever met."

He raised an eyebrow. "Only one of them?"

"If you haven't noticed, I'm attracted to your brothers, too." I grabbed him over top of his boxers. "The scar doesn't stop me from fucking you or from putting your dick in my mouth. I like you the way you are."

He groaned after I finished, and before I could comprehend what was happening, he lifted me over his shoulder and dragged me over to the sofa.

"Not on the couch," Dante shouted. "She's fucking bleeding."

"I don't give a fuck," Angelo fired back.

I giggled as his lips hovered over mine. "Daddy doesn't like when we talk back."

"Stop calling me Daddy," Dante growled. "I'm not even old enough to be your father. And get the fuck off that couch before you ruin the leather."

I puckered my lips. "I'm so bad. Come punish me, Daddy."

Dante scrubbed a hand across his jaw. "I'm gonna fucking kill her."

Angelo laughed in my ear. "Daddy's going to spank you for being a bad girl." He pushed up my dress and bent forward to kiss my stomach. "You know he gets mad when you challenge him."

"Good." I moaned as Angelo kissed his way up to my breasts. "I like it when Daddy spanks me," I said with my eyes on Dante. "I like it when he calls me a little slut and bosses me around." I raised my hand to beckon Dante. "I'm ready for my spanking, Daddy."

He shook his head, arms folded over his chest. "Lo, that's enough. Get off her!"

"Nah, I'm good right here."

Angelo stripped off my panties, throwing them on the floor with the bloody toilet paper that served as my makeshift pad. I was horrified. Yet, he didn't seem to give a damn. Nothing ever bothered Angelo.

Just his scar.

He looked at Dante. "You can watch me bury my cock in Ava's bloody pussy."

"Angelo, we should probably do this somewhere other than the couch." I hooked my arms around his neck and kissed him. "It's going to be all over the place."

"I was going to get another couch, anyway."

Stefan put his knee on the arm of the couch and gripped me beneath my arms to move me toward him. He fisted his cock. "Wrap those pretty lips around me, *bellezza*."

I opened my mouth for Stefan.

Dante gripped the back of the couch and leaned over us. "Need I remind you of the consequences for showing up late for work, Miss Vianello?"

"I'll be at my desk by nine," I choked out as Angelo entered me in one hard thrust. My eyes slammed shut as his piercings rubbed my inner walls. "Oh, God, Angelo."

Every time I felt the metal, I lost my damn mind. It was unlike sex with anyone else. His brothers fucked me good, but Angelo's big pierced cock massaged me in all the right places.

I bit my bottom lip while keeping my focus on Dante.

Furious, his nostrils flared. "If you're late, I'm chaining you to my balcony for the night. No more spankings. You won't like the punishments I have planned for you."

He stormed out of the apartment, slamming the door behind him.

"Daddy's going to kill you," Angelo taunted with laughter in his tone, slamming into me with force. His eyes darted between us so he could look at my blood on his skin. "But that's because he doesn't know what he's missing."

Stefan pinched my nipples. "Dante needs to fuck you, baby. Then he'll calm down." He grunted, forcing more of himself down my throat. "Fuck, your mouth feels good."

I could feel Stefan in the back of my throat as Angelo's big dick stretched me out in all the right places. My cum and blood dripped out of me and onto the couch each time Angelo pumped into me.

Angelo and Stefan seemed to be going for a sprint rather than their usual marathon. And they didn't last long.

After Stefan came, he wiped my lips with his thumb. "You're such a good girl."

"Our good girl," Angelo said before he collapsed on top of me, coming so hard it spilled out of me. "I don't give a fuck about periods. You wanna fuck when you're bleeding, come to me."

He pulled out, and a mixture of our cum and blood coated the dark leather. Angelo spread my legs with both hands and smirked. He lifted me so Stefan could see the mess he had made.

Like he was proud.

Angelo was so weird.

He stroked his dick coated in my blood. It stained his piercings, and I wondered how he would clean all of the blood.

"Do you have to take out the barbells?"

His golden-brown eyes pointed down at me. "Yeah, it's no different than when we fuck. You get all over me, baby. And I love it."

He bent forward and licked my pussy, flicking his barbell over my clit.

Stefan stroked his dick that was getting hard again, his eyes on my pussy. "Move out of the way, Lo."

Before I was about to cum again, Angelo stopped eating my pussy. He looked like a vampire after a feeding. Seeing so much of my blood on his lips, chin, and cheeks was kind of disturbing.

It didn't phase him one bit.

Angelo wiped his mouth and then moved off the couch so Stefan could replace him.

Stefan lifted my left leg over his shoulder and slid into me without giving me time to adjust to his size. He kissed my inner thigh and fucked me, his pace quickening with each thrust.

Meanwhile, Angelo stood next to me and played with his dick, enjoying my blood all over his skin. He looked excited by it. Like seeing so much blood was getting him off. Even Stefan kept glancing between my legs like it had the same effect on him. And here, I thought most men steered clear of periods.

Not these two.

They came again.

This time, Stefan filled me with his cum as Angelo coated my stomach.

Angelo stroked his dick until he got out every last drop. "I think we just found our new addiction, Stef."

Stefan nodded as he pulled out, staring at his dick. "Fuck, yeah."

Chapter Eight

AVA

D ante strolled into my office with a swagger in his step, stopping in front of my desk. "Have you prepared the second set of dummy accounts?"

I lifted a folder from the desk and handed it to him. "They need your approval."

He flipped through the documents inside the folder, his unreadable expression giving away nothing. I could never tell what he was thinking. Was he happy with my progress? Did he even appreciate the risks I was taking laundering money for his family?

Probably not.

He only saw me as his employee, another person who did his family's bidding. But was that true? I wasn't sure what to make of my relationship with the Luciano brothers.

Dante set the documents on the desk and removed a felt tip pen from his pocket. He signed off on each transaction. At least I wasn't the only one who would go down if this didn't work.

He handed the folder to me. "Send them to the bank, and then meet me outside the laundry entrance."

"I'll need about twenty minutes for the bank to approve the transactions."

Dante left the room without a word.

After dealing with the bank, I took the elevator to the ground floor. The Portofino offered in-house dry-cleaning and laundering for their VIP guests. And as I approached the back of the hotel, I could smell the dry cleaning chemicals.

Dante waited by the door. "Did everything go through with the bank?"

"Yes. All good."

He swiped his keycard on the digital wall scanner and extended his hand toward the double doors opening for us. I entered the steamy room with his hand on my back.

"Keep moving, Miss Vianello." His lips were so close to my ear as he bent down, creating tiny bumps along my skin. "Don't stop until you hit a dead end."

Gulping down my fear, I swallowed the lump forming at the back of my throat. I hadn't spent much time alone with Dante. And those few encounters were not that pleasant.

One of those times, he was carving a man's flesh and using turpentine as an antiseptic to make it hurt more. My limbs trembled thinking about what he would do to my family. He would probably make it the worst pain imaginable until we begged for our deaths.

So I devised a new plan to help us get out from under the Lucianos. I figured if they got their money back with interest, they would consider forgiving my father's stupid actions.

After talking with my dad, I felt he would run. The stress was becoming too much for him. He was only thinking about our escape plan. So instead of helping my dad embezzle more money—which would get us killed—I had a better idea.

For the past week, I had been taking cents on the dollar from every dividend check and reinvesting them into global markets. None of our clients would notice a few cents here and there. But after I added it up, I was able to invest over two million dollars into a new account.

Dante had already approved the dummy accounts. So he would be none the wiser when he saw them gaining value.

Besides, he didn't understand the numbers well enough to follow my paper trail.

He was smart.

But I was smarter.

Now that I had real feelings for the Luciano brothers, I didn't want to steal from them. So I let the hedge fund clients contribute to my scheme. These men were so wealthy they wouldn't even notice. While going through the books, I spotted a few familiar names. Men who were titans of industry. All of them connected to the Boardwalk Mafia.

Wellington Pharmaceuticals
Salvatore Global
Battle Industries
Atlantic Airlines
Mac Corp

Five publicly traded companies worth billions of dollars. When I looked them up, I noticed all the families lived in the same town called Devil's Creek. It was off the coast of Connecticut, not far from Hartford.

I wondered what tied them to the Lucianos, apart from one obvious link—the Salvatore family.

The Salvatores were cousins of the Luciano brothers on their mother's side. They ran Salvatore Global, which specialized in private security and trading. Two of the Salvatore brothers weren't blood related to the other two and had inherited their parents' airline.

Drake Battle was a tech genius in the news for his cutting-edge artificial intelligence software. I had owned shares in Battle Industries before my dad liquidated my portfolio. Mac Corp was a global shipping company owned by the Cormacs.

The Wellingtons were even more well-known than the others and the second wealthiest family in the world. Everyone in the United States used products made by Wellington Pharmaceuticals. That morning I had used a lotion from one of their subsidiary brands. They made everything from cold medicine to skin care products and vaccines.

So that was my plan.

To take small amounts from people who wouldn't notice the missing money. I would eventually replace the funds with the gains on my investments. In the end, it would all work out.

I hoped.

It was still a gamble.

Dante swiped his keycard on the wall scanner when we hit the dead-end at the back of the industrial laundry area. He entered a four-digit number into the keypad. I noticed he only used the extra layer of security for rooms that held money.

He opened the door for me and tapped on my back to push me inside. It was pitch black, further intensifying my anxiety until he flicked on the lights.

Inside the large room was a chute on the wall that looked like something you would see at a bank. Dante grabbed my arm and steered me over to it. "The money you drop from your office comes here."

Dante trusted me more than I thought. Otherwise, he wouldn't have shown me their operation.

"So someone waits down here to collect the cash?"

He bobbed his head. "We use our associates to recirculate the cash through the casino."

"The irony of your money washing room being at the back of the laundry is not lost on me." I grinned, but he didn't seem the least bit amused. "How come I don't bring the money here? Why use the chute?"

"Because we can't risk having anyone know you're helping us."

"Why? Don't you trust your men?"

"I don't trust anyone." He stuffed his hands into his pockets and studied my face. "It's best to keep each stage of the operation separate to mitigate the risk."

"Makes sense."

He clutched my wrist and pulled me toward another door at the back of the space. This room didn't require a keycard or passcode.

When he flicked on the light, a gasp escaped my throat. It stunk of bleach and a chemical I couldn't place. The scent smacked me in the face, choking me. I sucked in a few deep breaths and blew them out as I scanned the room.

They used this place to torture people.

Metal hooks and chains dropped from the ceiling and dangled from the stone walls. It appeared they tried to clean the blood from the floor and walls.

I spun around to leave, and Dante blocked my path.

"Dante, I don't want to be in here." I tried to step around him, and he moved with me. "Please. The smell is bothering my asthma."

His fingers gripped my chin, forcing me to look up at him. "Now, do you understand what goes into our operation?"

He was acting too calm and in control. This was a threat, his way of reminding me of what was at stake.

"Yes," I choked out. "I get it."

Dante released his grip on me so I could rush out of the room. I dodged hotel staff in the laundry area with Dante on my heels. They didn't even look at us, afraid to make eye contact. Dante had that effect on everyone.

I walked past the loud machines and didn't stop until I was in the hallway, where I could breathe again. Reaching into my purse, I removed my inhaler and took a puff. Before moving into the Portofino Hotel, I only used my inhaler once a month. And it was usually because of stress from school.

"You can go back to your office," Dante said as we headed toward the hotel entrance. "On Sunday night, I'll meet you to collect the money from the clubs. Don't be late."

That was a few days away. So I assumed I would get a reprieve from Bossman until then.

"I won't," I said before we parted ways.

My dad popped his head into my office and shoved his fingers through his black, scruffy hair that looked unwashed. He needed to get his shit together.

"I'm heading home for the day," he said with his eyes on the floor. "I'll see you in the morning."

"Okay." I rose from the chair and met him at the door. "I'll walk you to your car."

His gaze flicked to the security camera in the room's corner, then back to me. "Enzo is making chicken cacciatore for dinner," he said on our way to the elevator. "You should come home. Eat with us."

"I can't tonight. But will you tell Angelina and Enzo I say hello, and I miss them?"

He pressed his lips together and nodded.

We rode the elevator to the ground floor in silence, and he didn't push me for an explanation. I wasn't allowed to leave the casino without notifying one of the brothers. Besides, I didn't want to do anything to piss off Dante until my plan came to fruition.

Once in the parking garage, Dad stopped beside his car. It was a reserved space on the ground floor about twenty feet from the door.

"Ava, please be careful around them," he whispered, avoiding the camera's view. "You're too comfortable with the Luciano brothers. They are using you to get information."

"Dad, I know." I patted his shoulder. "I got this covered. Trust me."

"I trust you." He hid his mouth with his hand as he spoke. "But the Vitales want their money. And I don't have all of it."

"Will they tell the Lucianos now that their families are merging?"

His shoulders rose a few inches. "I don't know. I'm surprised Salvatore is even entertaining the idea of this marriage."

"Why?"

"He was going to kill Vincenzo Vitale after Carlo attacked Angelo. And then, he dropped it for some reason and agreed to split the city into territories." He scrubbed a hand across his jaw. "Salvatore has been getting softer over the years. I think he wants out of the Mafia to focus on the casino business."

"His sons don't understand why he's making Nico marry Vittoria."

"Because it doesn't make sense." He opened the car door and sighed. "Anyway, I better go before they spot us on the security feed."

Pushing my hands onto my hips, I frowned. "We're allowed to talk to each other, Dad."

He got inside the car and looked up at me. "I'm sorry for everything, Ava. I hope one day you can forgive me."

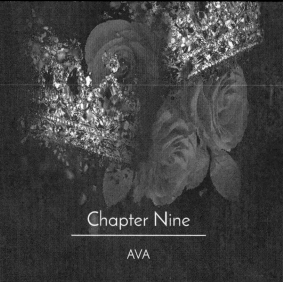

Chapter Nine

AVA

I came home to find Nico sitting in my living room. Like this day didn't already suck enough.

"Last time I checked, you don't live here." I set my purse on the table. "Why are you here, Nico?"

He pushed up from the couch, closing the distance between us. "To talk." Nico shoved his fingers through his blond hair, those pretty blue eyes aimed at me. "I need to apologize for the dinner. And for not telling you about the engagement. I'm sorry for a lot of things."

I followed the scent of garlic and spices into the kitchen. On the marble island, there was a silver room service platter. I lifted the lid and breathed in the delicious smell of a five-layer lasagna with a side of garlic bread.

"It's for you." Nico moved beside me. "Dante made you work all day. You must be starving."

I couldn't hide the smile tugging at my mouth. "Thank you." I sat on the stool and dug into the steaming hot food, speaking between bites. "But this changes nothing between us."

Nico sat on the stool beside me and watched me eat, tapping his fingers on the counter. "Ava, I'm sorry. When I took you to dinner, I wasn't engaged. I was hoping my dad wouldn't make me marry Vittoria. It wasn't a done deal."

"And now it is."

"I don't like her." Nico swiveled the chair to face me. "I'm sure as fuck not going to sleep with her. It will be a marriage on paper only. You can still be in my life. This doesn't have to be the end."

"Yes, it does. I'm not having sex with a married man. I don't want to be the woman you sneak off to see when your wife isn't around. That's not what I want." I chewed my food and set the fork on the plate. "Do you know what makes this situation even more fucked up?"

He shrugged. "No, what?"

"I like you, Nico." I shook my head. "At least I did before the announcement. Now I can't even stand to be in the same room as you." Biting back the tears pricking my eyes, I lowered my head. "You betrayed me. I was stupid to think we could have a future."

He put his hand over mine on the counter. "We still can."

I slid my hand off the table and put it on my lap. "No, we can't. Whatever was happening between us is over. It has to be the end."

"I like you, too, Ava." He traced his bottom lip with the pad of his thumb as his eyes met mine. "But I also think it's unfair that you're holding me to a higher standard when you're fucking my bothers. I never said anything about that. And to be honest, I don't care."

"Not like you have a say in who I fuck."

He gripped my knee. "Need I remind you that you're not here by choice? You are still our captive. And we have treated you like a queen. So don't give me that fucking attitude."

I slid off the chair, walked out of the kitchen, and headed toward the spiral staircase. Before I could put my foot on the first stair, Nico wrapped his arms around me from behind. He held me against his hard, muscular chest.

"You belong to the Boardwalk Kings," he breathed in my ear. "Which means you're mine, too."

"Nico," I whispered, hating myself for loving the feeling of him pressed against me. "Let me go. Please."

We stayed that way for a solid minute before he released me from his grip, stepping back from me. "I'll give you space, *passerotta*. But you're mine. And you're done when I say."

Breathing harder than usual, I closed my eyes and waited until I heard him leave the living room.

I wanted revenge. So I knocked on the twin's penthouse door. Angelo didn't have to leave for the club for another hour.

The door flung open after the second bang.

Angelo stood in the entryway, dressed in black track pants, shirtless. "Hey, beautiful." He leaned against the doorframe, his eyes drifting up and down my body. "To what do I owe the pleasure?"

I wore a black silk robe with nothing beneath it. So I tugged on the belt holding it closed and gave him a good look at my naked body. "I want to pay Nico back for not telling me about his engagement. And I need your help."

Angelo pulled me inside and carried me over to the dining room table. "Say no more. You know how much I love fucking with Nico. And fucking you."

He shoved down his pants and boxers and kicked them to the side. His dick was already hard and looked even bigger with all the piercings. I licked my lips at the sight of him. It felt so good having the metal rubbing my inner walls.

He stroked his length and pressed down on my stomach. My back hit the wooden table, and I propped myself on my elbows.

I pushed out my palm. "Wait, you have to film it."

Angelo's mouth tipped up into a sly grin. "You're a dirty little slut. I like it." He picked up his phone from the table and started typing. "I'll do you one better. Nico can watch me defile your beautiful body in real-time."

He bent forward, and a crazed look flickered in his golden-brown eyes before his tongue rolled over my clit. I cried out from the sudden contact. He flicked his tongue ring. Then he went back to licking me straight down the middle. And when the metal moved inside me, it was pure fucking torture.

With his left arm raised, he held up the phone as Nico answered on FaceTime. I could see his face appear on the screen.

"I'm in the middle of something," Nico said with an annoyed expression on his handsome face. "I gotta call you back."

"I have someone who wants to say hello," Angelo held out the phone for Nico to see me. "Are you too busy now?"

"What the fuck?" Nico groaned. "Call me back when you're done."

"No," I interjected. "I want you to see what you're never getting again."

Nico sighed. "Ava, you know I'm sorry. I don't have a choice. I have to marry Vittoria."

Angelo sucked on my clit, and I moaned as he tasted me. I gripped the table's edge and arched my back, desperate for more of his tongue.

"Watch me, Nico," I whispered. "Your brother is so good at eating pussy." My fingers wove through Angelo's short, dark hair. "Mmm…"

His tongue darted inside me, licking every inch of my sensitive flesh. Like a starved animal, he devoured me.

"Fuck," Nico groaned. "You look good enough to eat."

"Are you watching porn, Nicodemus?" Dante's voice was deep and sexy but also filled with irritation. "Turn that shit off."

He turned the phone so that Dante could see me, and I could see him. I rubbed my thumbs over my nipples and whimpered as Angelo ate my pussy.

Dante stared at me without speaking for a solid minute, his jaw clenched. Of course, he was angry.

Shocker.

I licked my lips and maintained eye contact with Dante as Angelo feasted on my pussy. "Hey, Bossman."

Dante shook his head, nostrils flaring. "Still up to your slutty ways, I see. I let you out of my sight for an hour, and you're back to whoring yourself out to my brothers."

"Well, I tried to whore myself out to you. But you're no fun."

Dante didn't make a move to leave, so maybe he was going to watch. Nico was breathing harder, his chest rising and falling.

Angelo stopped licking me for a second to speak to his brother, his lips glistening with my cum. "When was the last time you had sex, Dante. Get over here and bury your under-used dick in her tight pussy before it falls off."

I couldn't help but laugh.

So did Nico.

"Fuck off!" Dante snapped. "All of you."

Then he disappeared from the screen.

"Get back here," Angelo yelled. "Watch our girl come for me."

"Yeah, come back," I whimpered.

"She's not our girl," Dante yelled from a distance.

"He's still in the room." Nico turned his head to the right to look at Dante. "Not happy, but he's here."

Nico plopped down on the couch and unzipped his pants.

"What the fuck are you doing, Nicodemus?" Dante growled. "We're working."

So his dinner meeting was with Nico.

"Give me five."

Nico lowered his phone, so I could see him stroking his big dick. My freaky boss took turns sucking on my clit and licking between my slit. Then he raised my left thigh over his shoulder and thrust two fingers into me. And he wasn't soft about it. One quick thrust made my eyes roll back.

I could hear Nico jerking off. Dante moved back into the screen and stood behind the couch, glaring at me.

On the verge of an orgasm, I took the phone and muttered, "Where's Stefan?"

"At Lucky's," Dante bit out.

"Call him," I moaned.

Nico added Stefan to the group FaceTime. His face appeared on the screen a second later.

"Oh, fuck, *bellezza*." Stefan rubbed his hand over his mouth and groaned. "Damn. Look at you spread out on our dining room table."

I licked my lips, running my fingers through Angelo's hair. "Come eat me."

"Baby, I wish I could." He shook his head and sighed. "I gotta leave in a few minutes to handle business. But wait up for me, okay?"

"Okay."

"No, not fucking okay," Dante hissed. "Miss Vianello has to get up early for work. If any of you degenerates interfere, you will all pay the price."

"Jesus, Dante," Stefan grunted. "What is your fucking problem?"

"He needs to get laid." Angelo lowered the phone to my pussy and licked me from front to back, tasting every inch of me. He made sure to flick the barbell on my clit, and I squealed. "You can't tell me you don't want to fuck her."

Nico grunted as he stroked his big dick. "Doesn't she have a pretty pussy?"

Dante didn't answer.

I moaned as I hit the peak of my climax, each tremor shaking through me with the violent force of a hurricane. After I came, Angelo dropped my leg on the table.

"You're so sweet." He wiped his mouth with the back of his hand and leaned forward to suck my nipple into his mouth. "I love the taste of your pussy."

Angelo slammed his big cock into me without giving me a second to adjust to his size.

"Angelo." My eyes closed with each thrust. "Oh, fuck."

He yanked on my hair and smirked. "My dirty girl."

"Let me hold the phone." I held out my hand. "I want to see your brothers."

He placed the phone in my palm, put his hand on my shoulder, and fucked me hard. The table shook each time he pumped into me like a maniac. Like he was trying to ruin me.

"Let me see your dick, Dante." I moaned as Angelo fucked me harder. "I still think about you coming on me. I want you to do it again."

"Momentary lapse in judgment," he fired back. "It won't happen again."

I smirked. "Yes, it will."

"Like fucking hell it will," he growled.

I screamed his name, then Stefan and Angelo, leaving out Nico on purpose. He was engaged and an asshole who led me to believe I was special to him.

So fuck him.

I came once, twice, screaming their names over and over until my throat was dry. Angelo slammed his cock into me, fucking me so hard I struggled to catch my breath.

But I was okay.

Nothing near an asthma attack, but I would need a puff of my inhaler afterward.

"Come for us," Stefan grunted into the phone. "Fuck, baby. I love watching you with my brother."

Our skin slapped together with each powerful thrust. Angelo was a ruthless savage, tearing me apart with his piercings. And it felt so damn good I didn't care. He had stamina, showing no signs of slowing down as he pounded into me until he came so hard his cum leaked down my inner thigh.

I'd completely forgotten about his brothers until Nico came into his hand. Stefan watched like a dog in heat, his mouth wide and practically panting.

Dante was in the same place behind the couch, gripping the leather as if he were going to rip it to pieces. He could deny how much he wanted me, but he was a liar.

"Show's over." Angelo ended the call and dropped the phone on the table. "I have to leave for The Monella Club soon." His lips trailed down my stomach. "But I'm not done with you."

Chapter Ten

DANTE

The bullet sailed past my father and hit my mom in the chest. Her head dropped onto my shoulder. Blood splattered across the car, my face, and my clothes.

So much fucking blood.

She was dead.

Dead.

Dead.

Dead.

Heart racing, I woke up to my alarm clock with the reminder of that horrific fucking day.

The worst day of my life.

Fourteen years of torture.

It was almost the same dream every night. My brain wouldn't allow me to forget my mother. So even when I wanted to put all the bad shit behind me, I could always count on the nightly reminder.

That was why I never slept.

When Ava asked why I was never home, that was the reason. Because the minute I was alone, the thoughts would drift back into my mind on repeat.

So I worked until I passed out.

I got out of bed and hit the button on my alarm to silence the beeping. It was rare I slept until the damn thing rang at five o'clock. Most nights, I was lucky to get a few hours before I woke up drenched in sweat.

I went through the motions of my usual morning routine—an hour-long workout in my home gym at five-fifteen on the dot, with no deviations. Then I cooked an egg white omelet with a side of turkey bacon. Exactly three slices, never more or less.

My brothers made fun of me for my ritual, but it soothed me. None of them had a clue what it was like to be me. The underboss of the Boardwalk Mafia. Casino and hotel manager. I had thousands of people working under me, and I didn't have the time or energy to waste trying new things.

After eating breakfast and showering, I stepped into the hallway to meet Ava. I assumed she would be late again. That girl didn't respect my time.

But she surprised me by standing beside the elevator five minutes before nine. She wore a red knee-length dress that hugged her curves, paired with a black cardigan. Her legs looked long and lean in black Louboutin heels.

Fuck, she looked good.

But I didn't have time for women. And yet, I was stuck with the thief's daughter for the foreseeable future. Well, until I could prove both of their guilt and get rid of them.

With her arms behind her back, Ava smiled. "Good morning, Mr. Luciano."

"You're on time," I commented as I hit the button to call the elevator. "Are you still up from last night?"

She shook her head, and her dark hair fell in front of her eyes, forcing her to tuck it behind her ears.

I tapped Ava's back to push her into the elevator when the doors opened. "Unlike when you spend time with my brothers, today you will work. All day and night."

She leaned against the mirrored wall and rubbed her red glossed lips together, drawing my attention to her mouth. "So I'm your shadow for the day?"

"Yes."

I had to look away.

She was too fucking tempting, and I didn't want her. The second we uncovered her father's deception, she wouldn't be breathing anymore. So there was no sense in getting comfortable with a dead girl.

"What are we doing today?"

"Whatever the fuck I tell you to do," I shot back as we exited the elevator on the ground floor.

"Well, aren't you a ray of sunshine in the morning," she quipped. "It wouldn't kill you to be nice to me."

I stopped in the middle of the hallway. "Let's get something straight, Miss Vianello. I'm not your friend or your fuck buddy. I'm your boss. And you're here to do a job for my family. Do you understand me?"

She inched closer to me, and I wanted to walk away. But for some stupid fucking reason, I let her invade my space.

God, she smelled good.

Like grapefruit.

"Do you know what I think?"

"I don't care what you think."

Ava giggled, unaffected by my attitude. "I think you're a very busy and powerful man, and you work too much." She moved her palm to my chest. "And I think you need someone to relieve your stress."

I hated that she tried to use sex to make me like her. That shit worked on my brothers, but it wouldn't fly with me.

I shoved her hand away. "Don't fucking touch me. You don't know what I want or need." I continued down the corridor toward the ringing bells and sounds of people winning, which annoyed me even more. "You're young. A little girl who's still trying to figure out what to do with her life."

"I'm not a little girl," she challenged with anger in her tone. "I'm turning twenty-two in a few weeks."

"Do you know what I was doing when I was your age?" I focused on the casino ahead of us, and she followed my lead. "I was running a crew of men and going to war for my family. And

65

I had two young boys to look after when I wasn't working. You don't even know the meaning of responsibility, Miss Vianello."

"Would you please call me Ava?"

"No."

"Dante," she groaned. "I hate when you call me that."

"I don't recall asking what you like. You're my employee. I am your boss."

"Yes, you've made that clear already." She scoffed, flicking her long hair over her shoulder. "Are you a robot? Jeez, it's like you only have one mode."

I wanted to kill her.

And fuck her.

Fuck, I hated her.

"Speak to me like this again, and you will see a side to me you won't like, Miss Vianello."

Maybe I was a bastard.

I could have been nicer and called her Ava, but I enjoyed annoying her as much as she pissed me off. Just looking at her infuriated me.

I steered Ava toward a dozen blackjack, craps, and roulette tables where the regulars played. They looked like they had been up all night, chain-smoking and drinking. You could always tell when someone was losing big. And since it was also part of my job to approve the markers, I knew many of these degenerates.

"This is the pit," I told Ava. "We have a dozen pit areas at the Portofino."

She glanced up at me. "That's a lot, right?"

I nodded. "The number of pits depends on the size of the casino. The Portofino is the largest casino in Atlantic City. It's my job to coordinate with each pit boss in charge of the game managers, dealers, and clerks."

"I hate the tension between us," Ava said softly. "I'm trying hard to make you like me."

"And that's precisely why I don't." Avoiding eye contact with her, I nodded at the pit boss. "Your neediness makes you look stupid and pathetic. Before you came to work for us, I wasn't under the impression you were either of those things. You have disappointed me."

I stopped in front of the computer at the desk, scanned my card, and entered my credentials. Ava stood beside me and watched with curiosity. She let me flip through the screens and check the logs for a few minutes before speaking again.

"We got off on the wrong foot. How can I fix this?"

She was a Grade A people-pleaser and reminded me of Nico.

I fucking hated it.

The bastard brother was always so desperate for our love and attention. He didn't even hesitate when our father asked him to marry Vittoria. Anything to make the old man happy.

Ava was the same way.

She went out of her way to gain my attention. But she was trying the wrong shit on me. I wasn't someone she could coerce with sex.

"Stop throwing yourself at me," I suggested as my fingers flew across the keyboard. "You could start there."

She stood still for a moment, and I wasn't sure if she was breathing. I didn't need her having another asthma attack on me. Few people were smoking, but the scent wafted in the air.

"I'm not a whore," she whispered. "I know that's what you think. But, even I don't know why I have been acting the way I have lately. It's like something inside me snapped the day of my graduation."

I stopped typing. "Why are you letting my brothers pass you around like a toy?"

I wasn't sure why I asked because I didn't care about the answer. But from the second I saw her with Angelo and Nico at dinner, then the twins in the hot tub, I wanted to know how she felt.

How she tasted.

And that wasn't good.

Why did they keep breaking my rules to fuck her? I warned my brothers not to put a hand on her. Yet, they couldn't seem to stay away. They were addicted to her, and I wanted to know why.

Call it curiosity.

Nothing more.

"Do you want the truth?" Ava said in a hushed tone.

I cocked my head at her. "That would be preferable."

"I like them." A smile lit up her face. "I never felt wanted by anyone until I met your brothers."

That wasn't what I was expecting.

Interesting.

I logged out of the computer system and stuffed the keycard into the inner pocket of my suit jacket. Nodding at the opening between the tables, I gestured for Ava to move forward. She strolled down the aisle, teasing me with her perfect ass. I hadn't been with a woman in a long time.

Didn't have the fucking time.

We repeated the same process with the other pit areas in the casino. When Vinnie Morelli noticed me, he flagged me over to his station.

"I think we got ourselves a card counter, boss."

Vinnie's eyes lasered on a dark-haired man dressed in an oversized sweater and dark jeans. He didn't look like he could afford his bets and kept upping the ante. The man was either a terrible player or trying to cheat us. Either way, he was about to get tossed from the casino.

"How do you know he's counting?" Ava asked.

"We use a computer vision system with facial recognition software to track the known counters," Vinnie explained. "He's not on the list, but I've seen him around a lot over the past few weeks."

"Is he doing something wrong?" Ava wet her lips with her tongue, and it was distracting. "What caught your attention?"

Vinnie tossed a hundred-dollar chip at Ava, which she caught with one hand. "All casinos use RFID radio tags embedded in the chips. It sends a signal from the chips to our software."

I took the chip from her hand and removed the knife from

my pocket. Then I slid the blade beneath the center of the chip to pop it open for her to see the RFID chip. "We track the movement of the chips."

Mouth hanging open, she looked at me, then Vinnie. "So you can track the chips you've given me over the years?"

He nodded to confirm, a smile on his lips. "You never cashed them."

"Nope." She returned his gesture, beaming with delight. "I like collecting them."

I stuffed the chip into my pocket. "The radio frequency lets us track how much each blackjack player is betting per hand and how much they cashed out. Most card counters don't have the money to make large bets. So they'll take some of their winnings home and come back over multiple sessions."

"Huh," Ava whispered. "That's serious dedication."

"They're fucking degenerates," I told her. "This is how these losers make a living."

"By scamming you," she muttered, watching the man over bet on his next hand. "Technically, it's not illegal to count cards." She peeked up at me with those big brown eyes. "Right?"

I nodded. "Yes, that's true."

"So you're not allowed to take their chips or detain them."

"Also true," I shot back. "But you forget who they're dealing with, Miss Vianello. That shit doesn't fly in my casino. You steal from me, and I break your fucking hands and legs."

Her eyes widened at my comment.

I said it to gain her attention, to make her realize there were consequences for stealing from my family. The Lucianos were the only Mafia family worth billions of dollars, and I planned on holding onto my legacy. Men like the asshole over-betting at the table across from us were like cancer. We had to cut them out, or they would infect others.

"So, what are you going to do to him?"

"I'm waiting until he cashes out." Vinnie shoved his hands into his pockets and looked down at her. "Then security will follow him to his car and ensure he never returns."

Rocking back and forth, she hugged her middle. "Oh."

She was naive and innocent, unaware of how the real world worked.

This was business.

Nothing personal.

Despite my no-touching rule, I put my hand on her shoulder. "Let's go. We have a lunch reservation. And I don't like to be late."

Chapter Eleven

AVA

We left the casino area and headed to a trattoria called La Cucina della Mamma. It meant Mom's Kitchen in Italian. I was dying to know if any of Dante's mother's recipes were on the menu.

A gorgeous blonde woman waited for us with a smile. "Good afternoon, Mr. Luciano."

She opened the door for us.

He nodded as he entered the restaurant.

At least he was nasty with everyone, and it wasn't just me. As a general rule, Dante seemed to hate everyone. It wouldn't have killed him to smile or be nice once in a while. But he wanted his employees to fear him.

The place had a rustic vibe and smelled like a brick oven. I tipped my nose up at the scent of garlic and herbs, and my stomach rumbled.

Delicious.

I hadn't gotten the chance to make breakfast because I was so afraid of being late for work. God forbid I kept Dante from one of his many rituals. That man had a time for everything.

I wondered if he made time for sex, then laughed on the inside. He was too uptight to have had sex lately. But, even if he had, I was willing to bet it was clinical and robotic. Just him going through the motions with some whore from one of their clubs.

The hostess led us to our booth at the back of the restaurant. It was impossible to see us back here with its high, rounded walls. All by design, I guessed.

Dante liked his privacy.

Before I could even think about what I wanted to drink, a brunette with too much makeup on her face appeared. She set Dante's glass in front of him, then a Diet Coke for me.

I raised an eyebrow, surprised she knew my order. But when I looked over at Dante, he shrugged. Nico had told me a while back they knew everything about me.

They even knew my bra size.

Nothing got past my captors.

I sipped from the straw and glanced across the table at Dante, who read *The New York Times* the waitress handed him. She didn't speak as if she were used to being non-existent. They went through the motions with an odd familiarity.

A minute later, the waitress set a pizza on the table, sliced it, and put plates in front of us.

Dante kept his eyes on the newspaper. After she left the table, he dropped the paper on the leather bench beside him and lifted a slice of pizza off the metal tray.

I followed suit and bit into the Brooklyn-style brick oven pizza that tasted like heaven. It was hands-down the best pizza I'd ever had in my life. A soft moan slipped past my lips as I chewed my food.

Dante narrowed his eyes at me.

"This is amazing," I said after I swallowed another bite.

He nodded, then went back to eating.

"Is this place named for your mom?"

Dante ignored my question.

Not much of a surprise.

"It's not like I'm asking for your social security number. A simple yes or no answer would suffice."

His jaw clenched as he glared at me. "I'm trying to eat my lunch and don't like to be disturbed with questions."

"Why are you so uptight all the time? I'm just trying to get to know you, Dante."

"I'm a very private person. And I don't like being bombarded with questions during the only moment of the day I have to think without someone bothering me."

I wiped my mouth with the cloth napkin and sighed. "Look, I'm doing illegal shit for your family." I lowered my voice to a hushed tone. "Things that could put me in prison for the rest of my life. I'm not complaining. But at the very least, you can talk to me like a normal person. I think I've earned even the smallest amount of your respect."

He finished another slice of pizza before he looked at me again. "Yes, the restaurant is named for my mother."

"She must have been an excellent cook because this is the best pizza I've ever eaten."

"My mother was originally from Sicily," he admitted. "It's an old family recipe passed down for generations."

"The gnocchi you made for us. That was her recipe, too?"

He bobbed his head to confirm.

"You must miss her."

Dante turned his head away from me and lifted the paper from the bench. As if I hadn't said anything, he went back to reading. Well, so much for having small talk with Mr. Personality.

I was lucky to get anything out of him. Stefan made it pretty clear their mother was a sensitive topic for Dante. She died in his arms when he was twenty-one.

The same age as me.

I couldn't even imagine what that must have been like for him. It explained why he was so harsh and closed-off from the world. No one knew anything about him. Even his brothers only got the bare minimum.

Dante drank a cup of espresso, and then we left the restaurant without speaking another word. He enjoyed the silence, while I couldn't stand it. We were opposites in every way. So I wasn't sure how we were supposed to work more closely. I also didn't understand why I had to shadow the manager of the hotel and casino when I was their money launderer.

For most of the day, Dante didn't speak more than a few words to me. Only when he had to explain his job or introduce me to the personnel. We spent half of the afternoon dealing with the casino business.

They had one more card counter after lunch. Dante said they would handle it the old-fashioned way.

Broken legs.

Around three o'clock, we switched over to the hotel side of the Portofino. Dante spoke to the managers and signed off on new bedding and other mundane things that required his approval. Everyone in the hotel knew him, but none of them spoke without him asking a question first.

I could see the fear in their eyes.

They knew who he was.

A made man.

Dangerous.

Most people lowered their heads or flashed closed-mouth smiles. At least a handful of the men we encountered looked familiar, and I assumed they were family associates. It made sense they would install their guys in security and managerial positions. This way, their employees would never step out of line.

I was dead tired and regretting wearing heels by six o'clock. And, of course, Dante didn't seem to be ready to slow down. He was like a machine, moving from one place to the next.

After a day of shadowing Dante, I was beginning to understand him better. He didn't have to speak much for me to see how much weight was on his shoulders. His brothers had it easy compared to him. I also didn't understand why he needed to manage the casino and hotel. Each side of the business was a full-time job.

No wonder he never slept.

We entered the high roller poker room that had a game in progress. Dante grabbed my wrist and pulled me to the side, keeping me out of the players' view.

He pressed his index finger to his lips.

I nodded and leaned against the wall beside him. The damn thing had to hold me up because I was exhausted and ready for a nap. I didn't understand how Dante could repeat the same shit every day. And I thought my days were long and hard.

At least I got breaks.

"The guy with the red hat," Dante whispered, "he's going to take the pot."

"How do you know?"

He smirked.

After the players placed their bets, the dealer drew the Ace of Spades and put it in the center of the table.

"What did I tell you?" Dante pushed off from the wall and walked over to the man with the red hat.

The man got out of his chair as Dante approached. He tapped Dante on the back like they were old friends.

I hung out in the corner of the room and watched Dante congratulate the no-limit Texas-Hold Em tournament winner. He raised his hand and flagged over several casino guards. They also spoke to the winner, then escorted him out of the room.

After everyone cleared out, Dante walked over to me with the usual swagger in his step. This man could melt a woman's panties right off her body. If only he smiled every once in a while. He always looked so miserable.

"The man you saw win the tournament." Dante tipped his head at the door. "That was Johnny Salamanca. He's won the World Series of Poker seven times. The Portofino is sponsoring him this year."

My eyes widened at his confession. He spoke more about a poker player than anything all day.

And that gave me an idea.

"I don't know how to play poker." I inched closer to him and licked my lips. "Will you teach me?"

Dante briefly considered my question, then shoved up his shirt sleeve to inspect his Cartier watch. "We have thirty minutes until dinner. I suppose we can fit in one hand." He raised an eyebrow as he looked at me. "Depending on how quickly you learn."

"I was the valedictorian of my graduating class. Poker will be a breeze."

He snickered as he pulled out a chair from the table. Then he nodded at it for me to sit. I was so shocked by his rare moment of kindness I stared at him for a second before taking my seat.

Dante grabbed a deck of cards from the table. He plucked two stacks of chips from the holder on the felt table and slid a pile in front of me. They were gray and worth five thousand dollars each.

Damn.

Well, it wasn't like he would let me keep the money if I won. So I decided to take a gamble. I wanted something from Dante that money couldn't buy.

When his gaze met mine, I stared at his full lips and pushed out my chest. His eyes lowered to my breasts that spilled out from the V-neck dress.

"How about we play for something other than money," I suggested.

His eyes narrowed on me. "Such as?"

I bit my lip to still my nerves, eventually finding my voice to ask for something so bold. "I want a kiss if I win."

He scrunched his nose as if the thought of kissing a woman made him want to vomit.

"Fine," he agreed after a moment of contemplation, confident he would beat me. "And if I win, you'll be my slave for the week."

I grinned so wide it reached my eyes. "I like the sound of that."

Dante folded his arms over his chest and shook his head. "No, you won't."

When I extended my hand for him to shake, he stared at it as if I were diseased. I got the hint and dropped my arm to my side.

"It's a deal," I agreed. "Now, let's play."

Dante sat in the chair beside me and shuffled the cards. "Since it's only the two of us, we'll have to play heads-up. I'll deal first. As the dealer, I put up the small blind. You'll post the big blind. Got it?"

I nodded. "Yes, but you'll have the upper hand as the dealer."

He dropped the deck onto the table and slid it across the felt between us. "Draw a card. Whoever has the highest will deal."

I lifted the first card from the stack and sighed. "Three of clubs."

He raised the Ace of Spades from the deck and smirked. Then he took our cards and reshuffled them several times. Dante found a rhythm with how he shuffled, explaining the rules of poker as he repeated some OCD type of ritual with the cards.

Man, he was weird.

This was the first time all day he looked happy and content. So I didn't interrupt him as he went on about the rules, even though I had a basic understanding. I liked games that involved strategy and skill, so poker was right up my alley. Although, Dante had the advantage by dealing first.

Dante tapped the deck on the table. "Normally, the person to the left of the dealer would put up the small blind, and the player beside them, the big blind. The big blind is equivalent to the current minimum bet. That's twenty thousand for this table."

"How much do you bet?"

"The small blind is half your wager."

I added twenty thousand dollars in chips to the center of the table, and Dante contributed ten thousand. Then he dealt each of us two cards.

He kept his cards low to the table so I couldn't see, his

expression unreadable. I had a terrible poker face and tried to hide my excitement at getting a pair of sevens.

Dante eyed up the chips in front of him and added forty-thousand dollars to the pot, raising the bet. He glanced at me. "What's it gonna be?"

"I'll call."

I matched his bet, and then he dealt the three flop cards. So now we each had five cards to use—the Queen of Spades, the Ace of Hearts, and the Seven of Diamonds.

Yes! Three of a Kind!

It was impossible to tell what Dante had by his facial expressions. He wore the same mask of mystery. So I couldn't tell what he was thinking, which only made me want to know him more.

"You can check or bet," Dante informed me.

"I'll check."

Dante added more chips to the pile before flipping the Six of Hearts onto the table.

Not a card I could use.

We now had six cards to choose from to make a five-card poker hand. Another round of betting ensued, where we each added more chips to the pot. It now totaled over one hundred thousand dollars.

Dante dealt the river card, the last of the game.

A Ten of Diamonds.

I thought I noticed a slight flicker in his eyes. The closest thing I had seen to a tell since we started playing. He must have had a good hand because any form of emotion from Dante was rare.

He flipped over his cards and smirked. "Boat," Dante commented with zero emotion in his tone. He must have noticed my confusion because he added, "I have a Full House."

Three aces and a pair of tens.

Well, fuck me.

"I only have a Three of a Kind."

Dante inspected his watch and rose from his chair. "I'm meeting someone for dinner. You're excused for the night." Then he leveled me with one of his hardened glares. "I expect you on your knees in front of the elevator on Monday morning at nine o'clock."

"What?" I gasped. "On my knees?"

He patted the top of my head, a sly grin tugging at his delicious mouth. "Like a good little slave."

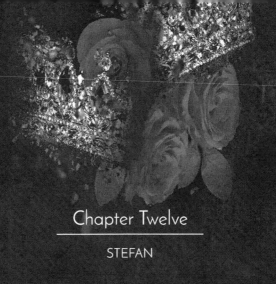

Chapter Twelve

STEFAN

I met Ava at the back entrance to Lucky's. She hopped out of the SUV and into my arms. We hadn't seen each other all week. Dante had been keeping our girl busy running errands and doing stupid shit his assistant could have done for him.

Tony Natale stood by the Range Rover, waiting until I raised my hand for him to follow us inside. He was one of my best men and loyal. There weren't many people we trusted with our girl and our money.

I held her hand as we walked down the dimly lit hallway. "I told the guys they can't smoke in my office. But if you don't feel good, let me know. I'll get you out of here."

"I have my inhaler," she said with a smile. "But let's hope I don't need it."

"You should be okay back here. We're far enough away from the smoky club."

After watching her gasping for breath at the engagement dinner, I didn't want to take any chances with her life.

She glanced up at me with those big brown eyes. "So, who's here tonight?"

I raised my shoulders a few inches. "Just a few of my guys."

"I noticed Angelo has men who hang out with him at The Monella Club. Is it the same for you?"

I nodded. "We're captains. Each of us has a crew working for us."

"How many people?"

"Twenty or so, give or take. We also have associates."

"How about Nico?"

Of all my brothers, Nico was the most forthcoming. He answered most of her questions without all the bullshit. It was rare he ever sugarcoated anything for her.

She hadn't even mentioned his name since the engagement dinner, but I could tell she missed him. He was the one she went to for everything. And now, I noticed she was leaning on me for support. I liked that she felt like she could tell me things because I wanted to know everything about her.

"He's a captain, too, right?"

I bobbed my head. "It's different with Nico. Paulie Amato is our father's *consigliere* and doesn't have a crew. He works directly for my dad, resolving disputes between the families. But since Nico is our dad's golden boy, he gets to be a captain without a crew. So he does his own thing and helps Paulie with whatever he needs."

"Is that why Dante hates him so much?"

For whatever reason, she was full of questions tonight. It must have been spending so much time with Dante this week. He rarely spoke, especially when he was working. My brother was so damn serious and uptight all the time.

"There's a lot of issues between them," I admitted, even though Dante would have killed me for telling Ava so much about him. "The shit with Nico's mom. His anger over our mom. It doesn't help that Nico doesn't have as many responsibilities as the rest of us. Especially Dante, who carries most of the weight."

"Is Paulie a lawyer, too?"

I shook my head. "Nah, he worked his way from the ground up. Paulie started as a runner when he was in middle school. His dad was my grandfather's bodyguard. My dad trusts Paulie like a brother. And Paulie needs Nico to help him with the legal shit."

We passed a handful of doors, but my office was at the far end. My family had a lot of security at the casino and our clubs. And as we moved down the corridor, cameras followed us. No one could get in or out of here without me knowing.

As we walked into my office, our conversation ended. The room had a large mahogany desk with couches to our right. Two men dressed in suits drank from bottles they raised to acknowledge me. I only let a handful of my guys hang out at the club.

"Ah, fuck. The boss is here," Pete joked. "Better put the blow away."

"You better not be doing that shit in my office," I snapped.

"Just fucking with you, Stefano." Pete Morelli dragged a hand through his dark hair and grunted. "Chill."

"They know I hate drugs," I told Ava before walking over to them, a frown in place. "And these assholes like to fuck with me."

She crept up beside me, her voice a whisper. "Doesn't your family sell drugs?"

I snapped my head at her, eyes narrowed. "Fuck, no. Who told you that?"

What a way to insult a guy? I mean, for fucks sake. Like my family would ever reduce ourselves to that low-level garbage.

Ava bit her lip, looking cute as fuck as she struggled to find the right words. "I just thought…"

She thought all Mafia families sold drugs.

"Nope, we have legitimate businesses, *bellezza*." I rubbed my palm over her tight ass and squeezed. "That's street shit."

Ava tipped her head back and laughed. "Yeah, that's why you need me to launder your money. Because you're so legit."

"Oh, this is the girl?" Vinnie had a deep smoker's voice. "The smart one."

I hooked my arm around Ava. "Yep. This is my girl. And if I see any of you sleazy motherfuckers even look at her wrong, I'll put a bullet in your skull."

She leaned into my embrace and gave me a cute smile. "Are you going to introduce me to your friends?"

"I was getting there, woman." I wrapped my arm around her middle and held her back against my chest. "This is Ava Vianello." I pointed at a big man with dark brown hair. "And that's Vinnie Corallo."

Her eyes widened, so I figured she'd heard of Vinnie "The Knife" Corallo. People whispered about how he was as sharp as a knife and could kill with just as much skill. I needed men like Vinnie on my side.

"You already know this *mezza sega*." I nodded at Tony and laughed. "Tony Natale."

"Who the fuck are you calling a lightweight?" Tony growled.

It was a joke because Tony was massive. Like a brick wall of muscle. He protected Ava each week when she collected the money from the clubs.

"You remember Pete Morelli, right?" I moved my hands to her waist and rubbed her hipbone with my thumb. "Nico said he took you to a party at his apartment."

She waved to Pete. "Hey."

He tipped his head at her. "Sup, girl."

"Don't say sup to my woman. Show some fucking respect. You sound like a gang member when you talk like that."

Pete laughed. "My bad, Stef." Then he looked at Ava with a mischievous look. "I was only joking. Apologies, Miss Vianello."

She elbowed me in the arm. "You don't have to get all possessive of me."

I bit her neck, my hand inching down her right thigh. "Baby, you're mine to possess."

"Stefan, not in front of an audience."

"Still shy, I see. We'll break you in eventually."

"We got an issue," Vinnie said with a sour expression. "Johnny Z poached a few of the girls. He's got them working over at The Red Lounge."

Johnny Z was short for John Zabatino. He ran a small operation on the other side of Atlantic City and owned strip clubs and bars. He didn't have the power of my family or even the Vitales, but he was still a constant pain in my ass.

I gritted my teeth. "That *pompinaro*. It's always fucking something. Which girls did he take?"

"Carrie, Tonya, and Quinn," Vinnie said.

"They're our best earners," Pete added. "We're losing thousands a day they're not here."

I snapped my fingers. "Tone, take Ava to The Monella Club and meet us at Johnny Z's place."

Tony nodded. "Sure thing, boss."

Ava spun around to look at me. "Why do you have to leave so soon? I just got here and haven't seen you in days."

"Baby, I gotta go knock some heads around." My knuckles grazed her cheek. "And you don't need to be there for that. Besides, I can't have any of Johnny Z's crew finding out about you."

I moved across the room, unlocked the safe, and dumped wrapped bills into a duffle bag. Tony took it from my hand and slung it over his shoulder.

Ava inched toward the door, and I grabbed her from behind and pulled her curvy body against mine. "Think about me when you're playing with Angelo," I whispered against the shell of her ear.

She tipped her head back and smiled. "Maybe I'll ask Angelo to film us so you can watch it later."

"My bad girl." I kissed her cheek and then shoved her toward Tony. "I won't be home until morning. So don't wait up."

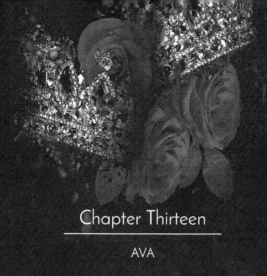

Chapter Thirteen

AVA

I kneeled on the floor beside the elevator five minutes before nine. Dante exited his apartment one minute later. Of course, he was early. Bossman valued punctuality.

Keeping my head down, I stared at his expensive Italian leather dress shoes.

He hit the button on the wall, and the doors opened. "Get up, little slave. It's time to work."

I rose from the floor, and Bossman pushed me inside the elevator. Dante got in beside me, ignoring me until we were on the ground floor. He acknowledged the guards posted up at various places down the corridor. Because this was their family's private entrance, there were always at least five men on duty.

Dante stopped when we reached the entrance to the casino and turned to look at me. He gave me one of his usual arrogant smirks, then dropped a set of car keys into my palm. "Take the Ferrari over to the dealer. Tony will bring you back to the Portofino."

I clutched the key, staring at him in shock. "Are you serious? You want me to do errands for you?"

He tipped his nose up at me. "What else would I do with a slave?"

I was an idiot for thinking it would be sexual. Dante made it crystal clear he wanted nothing from me. I wasn't even allowed to touch him without his permission.

"Okay," I groaned. "I'll be back soon."

Bossman walked away without another word. Straight and to the point. He wasn't a man who wasted time on small talk.

The Luciano brothers parked their cars by the loading dock when they didn't want to go through valet. So I knew where to find Dante's gorgeous Ferrari Portofino. It was a red convertible that cost a pretty penny but looked like it was worth every cent.

I didn't have a damn clue how to drive his car. So when I saw Tony standing beside Pete Morelli, I breathed a sigh of relief.

"You look like you're going to piss yourself." Pete laughed as he sauntered over to me. "I'd be afraid to drive Dante's car, too, if I were you." He opened his palm, wiggling his fingers with a cocky grin on his face. "Hand over the key, beautiful. I'll take it from here."

"If you're here to deal with Dante's car, why did he send me?"

"To test you." Tony crossed his big arms over his chest, making him appear even larger. "He likes to do that to new people." He opened the back door to a black G Wagon for me as Pete got into the Ferrari.

I sat in the back and watched Pete peel away from the building. Dante probably would have killed him for that. But Pete didn't strike me as someone who followed orders well.

Bella had mentioned the possibility of marrying Pete. I could already see the two of them challenging each other. She was a good match for him. Though, I wasn't so sure he was ready for her. My best friend wasn't what people expected.

Tony drove in silence to the dealership, which was in Edison, New Jersey. That would have been nice to know before spending close to two hours on the road.

Dante was trying to wear me down.

I wouldn't let him win.

A fter four hours away from the Portofino, it was Dante's lunch hour when I returned. He was already seated at his usual booth at La Cucina della Mamma. I stopped in front of the table and glared at him. My mood was shit after that long ass drive.

"Sit or leave," he said without looking at me, his eyes on *The New York Times*, which was open to the Business section.

"I'm starving. Are we eating pizza again?"

He shook his head and folded the newspaper in half. "I'm having chicken cutlet. You can order whatever you want."

A moment later, the waitress put his plate on the table before him. She asked if he wanted anything else. Then he tipped his head at me.

"Can I have the Caprese salad and a Diet Coke?"

She bobbed her head.

After she walked away from the table, Dante cut into the chicken and stuffed a piece into his mouth. He ate half of the chicken before looking at me. "Why do you drink Diet Coke?"

I shrugged against the leather bench. "I don't like all of the sugar from regular soda."

"You shouldn't drink soda. It's bad for you. Full of chemicals and carbonation."

Our server set my soda in front of me with a heaping salad bowl and left without a word.

Business as usual.

"Have you spoken to your father today?" Dante asked with a smirk.

"No, why?"

"I haven't seen or heard from him." He set his fork on the plate and studied my face as if searching for a lie. "It's unusual."

"I'm sure he's just busy. We have a lot of payments to

disburse this week. I think he mentioned something about meeting with new clients."

Mostly lies.

At the end of the month, we handled the bulk of the distributions. But my dad hadn't said anything to me about new clients.

Dante was right.

It was unusual.

My father was a workaholic and never missed a day. Throughout my childhood, he put his responsibilities to the Luciano family above all else—including me.

"Hmmm…" Dante brushed his knuckles beneath his chin, aiming that haunting gaze at me. "Giancarlo didn't mention anything to me about new clients."

"I'm sure it's nothing. Just an oversight."

His eyebrows rose. "Yes, an oversight, I'm sure."

He said one thing, but his tone indicated another. This was the first time I sensed Dante was suspicious of my father.

Did he expect me to confess?

I ate my salad without exchanging another word with Dante. He went back to reading the newspaper until his cell phone rang. Annoyed, he rolled his eyes as he read the Caller ID.

"What do you want, Nicodemus?" His nostrils flared as he glanced down at the paper, holding the phone to his ear. "I'm eating lunch. You know better than to disturb me."

I couldn't hear what Nico said on the other end of the line. But I assumed it couldn't have been good for me. Because once something got Dante's attention, his head lifted. He glared at me with pure hatred, his mouth twisted in disgust.

"Yes, send it to me," he shot back. "I will deal with it."

A second later, he hung up and stuffed the cell phone into the inner pocket of his suit jacket. His eyes still burned a hole through me. And with the deafening silence hanging between us, I couldn't sit still.

My lunch threatened to make an appearance, the salad churning in my stomach. I couldn't stand the silence anymore, so I said something I was sure to regret.

"I can help ease your stress." I forced a smile. "Whatever you need, I will do it for you."

I wasn't talking about sex.

But I would have done anything to get Dante on my side, to make him like me. That annoying people-pleasing side of me was rearing its ugly head again.

"Why do you keep offering yourself to me?" Dante shook his head. "It's not the least bit attractive."

Despite his nasty comment, I held my tongue and answered honestly. "Because I like you."

He snickered. "No one likes me. They fear me. You would be wise to do the same."

"Well, I like you," I shot back. "I think you're used to pushing people away. It's a defense mechanism to isolate yourself from the world. You're not as bad as you want people to believe."

Dante blew out a deep breath. "What makes you think that?"

"Because I see the way you care for your brothers. You're also very good to your employees. They are paid well above the current rate for their positions."

"At the Portofino Hotel and Casino, we treat everyone like family."

That was the slogan for their business.

They treated guests like celebrities, with high-end everything at their disposal. This wasn't some shitty hotel you could book for a hundred bucks. The cheapest room at the Portofino was well over four hundred dollars per night. And that was the standard guest room.

It was a five-star hotel with Michelin-star restaurants. The Lucianos did nothing half-assed.

"Even me," I tossed back at my handsome captor. "You might not like me. But you gave me an apartment on the same floor as your family."

"The apartment was not my idea."

"Whose was it?"

He crossed his arms over his chest. "My father."

"Because he thinks of me like family," I pointed out. "And in some way, you must, too. Or I wouldn't be sitting here, eating lunch with you."

Dante grimaced at my last statement. "You can go now. Return to your office and work on the new dummy accounts for this week's transfers."

"So that's it? I'm relieved of my slave duties for the day?"

He nodded.

I rose from the bench, and he didn't dare a second glance at me. So I left the restaurant and took my sweet ass time walking through the casino.

I rode the elevator to the executive suites on the third floor. Fear crept down my spine, crawling over my skin like tiny spiders as I pushed open the door. My dad's monitor usually had the screen saver flashing.

But it wasn't even turned on.

This was a test.

Dante let me leave so he could watch me from a distance. So he could see how I would react to my dad not coming to work.

I turned my head away from the camera in the room's corner and breathed through my nose. One deep breath after the other to calm my nerves. If I had an asthma attack over this, Dante would see it. He was probably looking at me now.

Observing me.

It was all a game.

I composed myself and left my dad's office. My heart thumped in my chest, beating like a drum. If I didn't get a hold of myself sooner, I would need my inhaler. I was so worried about being late for Dante that I forgot it on the bathroom sink.

My attacks were usually triggered by someone smoking or wearing too much fragrance. But my panic was rising. Dad had fucked both of us when he let his greed control him. Let it dictate both of our lives.

He royally screwed everyone in our family—me, most of all.

His only daughter.

How could he do this to me?

We could have escaped this town if I were seven million

dollars richer. We could have gotten out from under the Lucianos. But no, he had to take every cent. The bastard didn't leave me a thing after years of teaching me how to invest.

I sat in front of my computer and logged into the accounts. The Lucianos were worth a fortune. I could see how Dad made the idiotic mistake of thinking he could replace the money before they would notice.

I was already working on getting the money back for them. Thankfully, Dante didn't know enough about the financial system to spot the small gains here and there.

I would buy our freedom.

It was a good plan.

But I needed time.

With Dad not showing up for work, I wasn't sure how much longer I had to return their money. But, just seeing the accounts gave me a sense of relief. I let out a few deep breaths and already felt my nerves settling.

I had broken several dozen federal and state laws. But, it didn't matter anymore because the possibility of getting murdered by the Luciano brothers kept me going.

I reached into my purse and grabbed my cell phone. Angelina answered on the second ring.

"*Mi amore*," she said with a sigh.

"Hey, Ang. I missed the sound of your voice."

"I missed you, too." She breathed into the phone, and a few seconds passed before saying, "Have you seen your father?"

"No," I whispered. "He didn't come to work."

"I was afraid this would happen."

"Do you know something?"

"I overheard him talking to someone on the phone last night. They were arguing about money. Two thugs came to the house an hour later and beat him bloody."

I turned my chair to faced the wall. With my back to the camera, Dante couldn't see my face. But he was probably listening to me.

"Who was it?" I whispered.

"Men who work for the Vitales."

No!

"What happened after they left?"

"Your dad packed a bag and drove off the property. We haven't seen him since last night."

I thought about the account in the Bahamas and the plane ticket he wanted me to buy. Was he going to the islands? And if so, where the fuck was he going? Until I could access his home safe, I had no way of knowing the plan in its entirety.

"Please come home, *bambina*," Angelina said in a hushed tone. "Your birthday is next weekend. Enzo and I want to see you."

"I'll be there," I assured her. "But I can't stay the night."

"We can have cake and ice cream and open presents," she said with delight. "I will see you then."

After we hung up, I stared at the wall for a solid hour, trying to control my breathing. Every year since my fourteenth birthday, I had dreaded the day. That was when Dad sent my mom away. It was the last time I saw her.

I hated celebrating my birthday.

Why would this year be any different from the others? My absentee father was on the run. My mom was at a wellness spa in California. It was another year I would celebrate with the staff.

Happy fucking birthday to me.

Chapter Fourteen

DANTE

A round midnight, my cell phone rang with a call from Nicodemus. He knew better than to disturb me after hours unless it was an emergency.

I slid my finger across the screen and raised the phone to my ear. "What, Nicodemus?"

"It's Giancarlo. Two of the Vitales' hitmen visited him last night. He left with a go-bag an hour later."

I sat up and slid my legs off the side of the bed. "What business does Giancarlo have with the Vitales?"

"I don't know," he breathed into the phone. "But he could be working with them. That would explain why he's been so jumpy around us. Maybe it's about more than the money he stole."

"It's time to accelerate our plans for Ava. She's caused too much of a disruption in our lives."

"No, don't hurt her," he pleaded. "Whatever Giancarlo is up to, it has nothing to do with Ava."

"We need information." I headed downstairs to the kitchen and grabbed a bottle of water from the refrigerator. "I'm done playing games with that girl."

"At least give Ava a chance to defend herself before you accuse her of wrongdoing."

"No," I snapped. "Her father is an enemy of our family. And by association, she's as good as dead."

"Then let me deal with her," he insisted. "Ava will talk to me."

"Not anymore." I slammed the refrigerator door. "You're engaged to Vittoria, and she hates you for it."

"Then let one of the twins talk to her," he begged. "Don't fucking hurt her, Dante."

"I'm the underboss," I reminded him. "You take orders from me. And if I tell you to put a bullet between her eyes, you will do it without questioning me. Do you understand me, Nicodemus?"

He breathed loudly into the phone. "Yes."

"Get some eyes on Giancarlo. Have our men track him down and bring him back to AC."

"I'll call you when I have an update."

I dropped the phone on the kitchen island and ran my fingers through my hair, tugging at the ends. Sometimes, I hated being the boss. But, it wasn't just the casino or the hotel. I had hundreds of men, soldiers in our army, who answered to me.

My father had put distance between himself and the men years ago. After my mother's death, he became more of a recluse. Paulie Amato was his *consigliere* and served as his middle man, while Nico handled the legal side of the business.

So instead of calling my dad, I dialed Paulie. He answered after several rings, his voice deep and groggy.

"Did I wake you?"

"No, it's okay, boss," Paulie muttered. "I'm awake now. What can I do for you?"

"Giancarlo Vianello is working with the Vitales. Do you know anything about this?"

"No," he admitted. "This is the first I'm hearing. Are you sure?"

"Yes."

"Okay." I heard rustling in the background and then footsteps. "I'll get some guys on him. What do you want to do about his daughter?"

"I will handle the girl."

"You should speak to your dad about Ava. Salvatore won't take too kindly to you whacking the girl without his permission."

"I won't hurt her. Not yet, anyway."

"Talk to your dad. I'll handle Giancarlo and the business with the Vitales."

I called Paulie first because I wanted someone to tell me Ava was a loose end. Just another person who fucked us over.

Why did everyone like her?

She was so annoying and clingy, desperate for attention and affection. I fucking hated it. And yet, I didn't completely hate her, which pissed me off even more.

"Wait until morning to tell your dad the news," Paulie suggested. "He hasn't been sleeping well and has been taking medicine."

"Is he okay?"

"Yeah, sure. He's just more stressed than normal. That's all. Not a big deal."

I thought it was odd Paulie didn't want me to call my dad. And then I wondered if he was hiding something. He had been with my family for a long time. But ever since he suggested the engagement to Vittoria Vitale to my father, I doubted his judgment as the family advisor.

He went behind my father's back to arrange a sit-down with Vincenzo Vitale. And he'd been taking unauthorized meetings outside the scope of his position. Nicodemus gave me daily updates on Paulie and his movements. The bastard brother was also suspicious and had voiced his concern to our father, who assured us we were paranoid.

Dad was too trusting of the people closest to him. Giancarlo had been his friend from childhood, and look at what that fucker did.

So we couldn't trust anyone.

Not even Paulie.

"Let me know when you find Giancarlo," I told Paulie. "I speak to him first. Understood?"

"Sure thing, boss."

After we hung up, I sat in the kitchen for another hour, thinking about what to do with Ava Vianello. My brothers were going to give me fucking shit over her. All of them were obsessed with her golden pussy.

That only left one option.

Chapter Fifteen

AVA

On my last day as Dante's slave, he stood in the entryway to my office and cleared his throat. I stopped typing and looked up from the computer screen. All-day, he ignored me, like I was a fixture on the wall. It wasn't as much fun being his slave as I had hoped.

He raised his hand to beckon me. "Come with me, Miss Vianello."

It was after five o'clock and a deviation from his usual quitting time. Dante didn't eat dinner until seven o'clock.

I got up from the desk and stood before him. "Where are we going?"

"To my apartment."

The penthouses were on the hotel side. So we had to take the elevator downstairs and walk through the casino. Dante didn't speak as we went through the motions. I was getting used to the silence and didn't mind it.

In some ways, it was nice. He didn't feel the need to fill the voice with white noise.

Not like his brothers.

Nico was chatty, and so was Stefan. Angelo was a mixture of his twin and Bossman. I was used to their personalities and understood what they liked. It was best to wait until Dante spoke to me. That seemed to cause the least amount of fights. Though, every time I opened my mouth, it angered him.

We got off the elevator and turned left. Dante lived in the apartment beside his father. Between the two sets of doors stood men with guns.

Dante opened his door and shoved me inside, guiding me through the house with his hand on my back. Unlike the twins' place, this was bright white and sterile—zero personality, which didn't shock me. The art on the walls was tasteful and modern. The space was decorated in various shades of cream and looked like a hotel suite.

He had the same open concept floor plan and the patio doors off the kitchen. The only difference between our penthouses was the bar on the right side of the dining room. Dante went straight for the wet bar and filled a glass with amber liquid.

Then he turned around, leaning his back against the wooden bar, and surveyed me with curiosity. Was he going to try to pry the information about my dad out of me? He had to know Dad was missing. It was the second day in my entire life he hadn't shown up for work.

It didn't go unnoticed.

Dante didn't miss a beat.

He dropped onto the leather couch and rested his dress shoe on the coffee table. I wasn't sure what to do, so I followed him. But when he looked up at me, eyes filled with rage, I stopped myself from sitting.

I stood up straight and slapped on a forced smile. "What can I do for you, Mr. Luciano?"

He drank from the glass, tapping his fingers on his knee. "You can tell me where your father has been hiding."

Nerves slid up the back of my throat, choking me. "Um," I bit out. "I honestly don't know."

He curled his hand into a fist and growled, "Bullshit. Where is he?"

I inched closer, careful to keep enough distance between us. "I'm telling you the truth," I muttered, my voice wavering. "I called home to see if he was there."

"And?"

I shook my head. "Angelina said he hasn't come home. I tried calling his cell phone, and it keeps going straight to voicemail."

"That *pompinaro*." His nostrils flared. "Where does he go when he's not working or at home?"

"He's worked seven days a week for my entire life. Your dad is his only friend. My mom is in California." I shrugged. "So I don't know. I have been in Manhattan for the last four years. If he got new friends, I don't know about them."

He scrubbed his hand across his jaw. "Friends like the Vitales?"

"I wouldn't know," I lied. "Your family is merging with theirs. Ask them."

"No, we're not," he snapped. "They work for us. The Vitales will never be privy to our operations. Your father has no reason to discuss anything with them."

I wasn't sure what I was thinking. But I wanted to distract him from asking the one question that would force me to lie. So I moved between his spread thighs.

He didn't yell at me.

Just stared at me.

I sank to my knees between his legs. "Dante, I don't know where he went. If I did, I would tell you."

He tipped the glass to his mouth. "Would you?"

"I would. You can trust me."

He didn't tell me to leave or shove my hands away.

"What can I do to make you feel better?"

"I don't want you to coddle me," Dante hissed. "Fuck off and let me drink in peace."

"I want to put your dick in my mouth and suck it until your cum slides down my throat. And I think you want that, too." I reached for his zipper, and he clutched my wrist, holding my gaze. "You're always worrying about everyone else. But no one does anything for you. So relax and let me take care of you."

He didn't answer.

Instead, he dropped his hand to the couch, let me unzip his pants, and whip out his big dick. Fisting his shaft, I licked my way up to the tip.

Dante didn't look away.

His lips parted as he watched me suck his cock. Then his hand moved to the back of my head, forcing me to take more of him. Like his brothers, he was so big my cheeks puffed out. I even gagged a few times when he pushed himself too far down my throat.

He groaned as if in pain, slipped his fingers through my hair, and pulled hard. When I looked up at Dante, his eyes were closed. A strange expression crossed his handsome face, split between pain and pleasure.

Dante probably hated himself for letting me touch him. Now he knew why his brothers kept coming back for more. I was hoping he would lower his guard and finally begin to trust me.

Technically, I hadn't lied to him.

Not yet.

So, for now, this was a good distraction. Maybe an orgasm would get Dante's mind off everything.

It was a challenge to fit all of him in my mouth. I could only suck about half of him at a time without feeling I would choke. And every time I made a gagging sound, he grunted. Dante yanked my hair hard enough to rip it from the scalp.

I found the perfect rhythm, and when his cock pulsed in my mouth, his eyes opened again. Dante pushed my hair behind my ear so he could watch me.

His grip tightened on my hair as his legs trembled. He was so close, seconds from coming. And when he came, he made the sexiest fucking sounds.

It was feral.

So hot.

Dante shoved his hand through his hair and groaned, staring at the ceiling. He looked so unhinged, but only for a moment. I loved seeing this side of him.

I couldn't move, frozen in place and breathing hard. He was doing the same, unable to speak. Not like he was going to talk, anyway. But our brief moment of silence was interrupted by his cell phone ringing.

All of their phones seemed to ring around the clock. It was like they never had a day off, which made sense why until recently, my dad never did. He was always on call, like them.

"Yes?" Dante said into the phone as he tucked his dick into his boxers. "No, I will handle it, Stef. "A beat passed. "Because I said so."

They spoke for another thirty seconds in clipped sentences unit Dante hung up with his brother.

He shoved the phone into his pocket. "When will my brothers grow the fuck up?"

"You don't have to shoulder all your family's burden."

I probably should have held my tongue. It wasn't my place to get involved with their family drama. And I wish I would have chosen this moment to keep quiet.

"Yes, I do," he said with an attitude. "If I don't, no one else will."

Since I went there with Dante, I decided to keep going. He looked less stressed than before I blew him.

"You don't give your brothers enough credit. They want to help you. We all do. So let us."

He zipped up and then flung out his hand. "Get out!"

I pushed myself up from the floor and wiped my mouth with the back of my hand. "What the fuck is your problem?"

"You are my problem." He finished the liquid in the glass and rose from the couch, now towering over me. "Go before I drag you to your apartment by your hair."

"Why are you like this?"

I was on the verge of crying, the tears pricking my eyes. But I fought my best to contain them. I didn't want Dante to see me look weak, to think I couldn't handle him.

"You wouldn't understand."

When he walked away to refill his drink, I left the apartment with tears spilling down my cheeks, regretting ever touching him. And he didn't come after me.

Chapter Sixteen

DANTE

A va thought she could play games with me. And she was getting way too comfortable with my brothers. So it was time to move on to the next phase of my plan.

No more waiting.

We'd had men out looking for Giancarlo for close to a week without success. Being nice to the thief's daughter wasn't getting us anywhere, and it was time to show her how we did business.

The old-fashioned way.

I ordered Angelo and Stefan to come home from the clubs. Of course, they weren't thrilled with my plan. Neither was Nicodemus. But I was the boss of this family, and my brothers would do what I told them.

With my brothers behind me, I opened Ava's apartment door with the master keycard. Whenever I wanted, I could slip in and out. This place wasn't a perk of her employment. It was a way for us to track her at all times.

She had zero privacy.

The lights were off on the first floor. And after the door slammed behind Nicodemus, Ava appeared at the second-floor railing. Eyes wide, she stared at us. Ava wore a black, silky spaghetti strap shirt that rode up her stomach and matching shorts.

"What are you doing here?" She put her hands on her narrow hips, pushing out her tits. "I'm getting ready for bed."

I crossed my arms over my chest and looked up at her gorgeous body, careful not to let my eyes wander too much. "You're coming out with us. Get dressed."

"But," she bit out. "Where are we going? It's close to midnight."

Angelo walked toward the stairs and extended his palm, staring at her. "Get dressed, *dolcezza*. It's a surprise."

Even with him speaking calmly, using one of his stupid pet names for her, she still looked scared. Her top lip quivered, despite her best effort to hide her fear from us.

She was wise to be afraid.

"What should I wear?"

"Something comfortable." Angelo threw out his hand. "Now, go."

"Um." Ava bit her lip, shifting her weight from one foot to the other. "Okay, give me a minute."

"I don't like this," Stefan said in a hushed tone. "This could kill her."

Nicodemus nodded in agreement. "If you hurt her," he warned but didn't get out the rest before I raised my hand to silence him.

"Enough. I don't care what you want. This is my decision."

Angelo leaned into my side and slid his arm across the back of my neck. "There are easier ways to get the information out of her."

"You can't fuck the answers out of her," I shot back. "Leave this to me. You can stay behind if you're too much of a pussy to follow through."

Angelo gritted his teeth as our eyes met. "Not a chance. I don't trust you alone with Ava."

"Neither do I," Nicodemus added.

Stefan bobbed his head to agree.

Fuck them.

I make the rules.

Ava appeared a few seconds later, dressed in black yoga pants, designer sneakers, and a tight black tank top.

Perfect.

She would get dirty where we were going.

Stefan curled his arm around Ava and led her to the front door. Since she was still mad at Nico, Stefan was her second choice to find comfort. She would never find it in me. And Angelo was too fucking unhinged to make anyone feel better.

We rode the elevator to the ground floor. I hopped into the passenger seat of the G Wagon parked by the loading dock. Ava sat between Nico and Angelo in the backseat. Whenever we were together, I always insisted Stefan drive. Angelo had too much road rage, and I couldn't tolerate looking at Nicodemus for long enough to give him the privilege.

"Will someone please tell me where we're going?" Ava asked. "The silence is freaking me out."

"It's going to be okay, *passerotta*," Nico said to assure her.

"Don't call me that. You're engaged. Save that name for your wife."

"You're still mine, Ava."

"Not anymore. But your brothers do a good job of keeping me company." She leaned into Angelo and put her leg over the top of his. "Isn't that right?"

"Yeah, baby." Angelo bit her earlobe and shoved his hand between her thighs. "You belong to the Boardwalk Kings."

Nicodemus grabbed her leg. "Which means she's mine, too."

Ava shoved his hand away. "I'm not a toy for you guys to play with."

I laughed. "Could have fooled me."

Ava slid her leg back to the floor and leaned between the seats. "You didn't mind playing with me earlier when I had your dick in my mouth."

"Wait, what?" Shocked, Stefan turned to look at Ava, then me. "You finally let her touch you?"

"Whores are here for one purpose. So it was only fair I let Miss Vianello do her job."

Gripping the armrest, she glared at me. "You're a horrible liar and a terrible person."

Stefan shook his head and snickered. "That's my girl."

Angelo rubbed her ass like it was a pat on the back. My fucking brothers were such assholes. They liked her too much, and that was a problem. If this panned out the way I thought it would, she wouldn't be breathing for very long.

"Don't encourage her," I snapped at them. "The three of you have let her off her leash for long enough. We wouldn't be here now if you had followed my instructions."

Ava sat back in her chair and rested her head on Angelo's shoulder. Nicodemus put his hand on her knee, and she pushed it away. They were pretty damn cozy unit the engagement dinner. Even with her acting like a little bitch, my idiot brother still wanted her.

What a fool?

They were all so misguided.

The twins had relied on my advice and parenting for more than half of their lives. And the bastard brother was always trying to win my favor. Nicodemus would have done anything to make me like him. But when it came to the girl, they wouldn't budge.

We drove for twenty more minutes before Stefan parked at the edge of the woods. It was pitch black out in the wilderness, the moon hidden by the trees.

"Where are we?" Ava whispered, her voice shaking.

I ignored her question and got out of the SUV. Angelo grabbed a shovel from the trunk, slinging it over his shoulder like a baseball bat. Ava stood frozen between us, her lips parted.

"What the fuck is going on?"

Nico laid his hand on her shoulder. "Remember when you asked if you'll ever have to help me dig a grave?"

"Yes," she croaked.

Nico tapped his fingers on her back. "Well, today is the day."

Her eyes widened as she looked up at him. "You can't be serious."

"Dead serious," Angelo added. "Now, let's go. Time to work."

Ava wrapped her arms around herself, unable to hide how much she trembled as we walked into the woods. I let my brothers do shit their way for a while.

My dad wanted me to get closer to Ava to make her feel more welcome and part of our family. But letting her shadow me at the casino was about as close as we would get.

Ava whimpered whenever an owl hooted, or a branch snapped beneath an animal's weight. Angelo put his hand on her back and guided her forward. She kept asking questions, none of which we answered.

About ten minutes into our walk, we stopped by one of many gravesites. You wouldn't know it by looking at the wooded area. But this was one of many places we buried bodies.

I gripped Ava's arm and curled her fingers around the shovel's handle. "Start digging."

Her entire body shook, causing her teeth to chatter. "No, I don't want to do this."

"You don't have a choice." I pointed at the ground in front of her. "Dig."

We reserved this type of punishment for our worst enemies. Our tradition was to make them dig their own grave. If we had to waste our time covering their bodies with dirt, digging the hole was the least they could do before leaving this world.

"Why aren't any of you helping me?" Her gaze shifted between us. "Why are you all standing there, staring at me?"

"Get to work." I stuffed my hands into my pockets and nodded at the ground. "The longer it takes, the angrier I will get."

Ava groaned as the shovel cracked the dirt. She had her back to us and sniffled, wiping at her face. Crying was not going to get her out of this situation. That shit didn't work on me, anyway.

I'd watched grown men drown in tears, begging for their lives. When I made up my mind, the decision was final. My father said I was a born leader because I could do the hard shit. I had no problem sentencing a man to death.

I had no conscience.

No remorse.

"Nico, help me," Ava muttered, glancing over at him. "Please."

He shook his head. "No can do. It's time to spread your wings, little sparrow."

She breathed harder, her hand flying to her chest. I couldn't tell if she was panicking or having another asthma attack. "But I need help." Looking at the twins, she sniffed back more tears. "Why are you making me do this?"

"No more talking," I warned. "Or I'll cover your mouth with my tie."

That shut her up.

Ava plunged the shovel into the earth and started making some progress on her gravesite. She whined and carried on, speaking to herself under her breath in Italian. Our names slipped past her lips as she cursed.

I didn't care if she hated me.

Nicodemus gave her his sad puppy dog face, shaking his head whenever he looked at me. He felt bad for her. Even Angelo was unhappy with me and was usually down for a bit of mischief.

They were getting too soft.

I didn't like it.

Over an hour passed before Ava finished making the world's smallest grave. It was maybe three feet deep and five feet across, barely long enough to fit her petite body.

With the shovel in hand, she spun around to look at us. "Okay, so who are we burying?"

"No one yet." I moved in front of the hole and crossed my arms over my chest. "You're not done."

"What do you mean?" Ava threw the shovel beside her and huffed. "I did what you asked of me."

"Six feet is the standard depth of a grave. You have a few more feet to go."

Her top lip quivered as she sucked in a deep breath. "But my arms hurt." She took another deep breath. "I need my inhaler."

Nicodemus knelt beside the grave and reached into his pocket. "I brought it for you."

She took it from his hand with a scowl. Then she took a puff of the medicine, holding it for several seconds before blowing it out.

"That's enough, Dante," Stefan said with fire behind his words.

Furious, I pointed my finger at him. "Shut your mouth. She's done when I say."

"What is all this about?" Ava asked. "Who are you burying here?"

I snapped my head at her. "You."

She inched backward, her eyes wide as she gazed up at us. "What? No." Choking on her words, she breathed so hard that her chest rose and fell rapidly. "I didn't do anything."

"The fuck you didn't." I stood over the grave and folded my arms over my chest. "Where is your father?"

"I don't know." She swatted at the tears falling down her cheeks. "I've been trying to reach him for days. I left him voice-mails, but he hasn't returned any of my messages."

Nicodemus had confirmed this earlier. So at least she was telling the truth.

I jumped into the hole with her, pressing her back to the dirt. "Why did he run?"

She tilted her head to the side, away from my face. I was too close for my comfort. My nose touched her cheek, and I hated the contact.

I wanted her to know I wasn't fucking around, so I wrapped my fingers around her throat and forced her to look at me. "You have one chance to answer truthfully. If you answer incorrectly, you will die in this hole. And when I find your piece of shit father, I'll throw his corpse on top of yours."

She couldn't breathe, so I loosened my grip, letting my hand fall to my side. Clutching her chest, she gasped for air. I couldn't tell if this was an act.

Was it panic?

Her asthma?

After the show she put on at Nicodemus's engagement dinner, I was convinced she was a better actress than she thought.

"Last chance, Miss Vianello. Why did your father run?"

"Because he stole a lot of money from you," she choked out.

"How much?"

Eyes downcast, Ava whispered, "Ten million dollars."

"And you didn't think to come to us?"

Sobbing, she put her hand over her heart and took a few deep breaths. Tears streamed down her cheeks, mixing with the dirt on her skin. "Look, I didn't help my dad. He asked me to cover it up for him. But I couldn't do it."

"Why not?"

"Because I have feelings for your brothers," she said with her eyes on her feet.

I slid my hand beneath her chin and tilted her head back. "I know you've been hiding something from me. What have you been up to?"

"I tried to get the money back," she said between strangled breaths. "Every penny plus interest."

My father was right about Ava being brilliant. In a short time working for our family, she was already outperforming Giancarlo.

Nicodemus hopped into the hole beside us and pulled Ava into his arms, molding her back to his chest. Then he put the inhaler in front of her mouth. "Just calm down, *passerotta*." He tucked the fallen strands of hair behind her ears. "Take a deep breath."

After her breathing returned to normal, Nicodemus swaddled her like a newborn baby. But I wasn't finished with my questions.

"How did you attempt to get back our money?"

"You probably won't like it," she muttered as she wiped the tears from her chin. "I wrote a program that takes a few pennies on the dollar from every client's dividend check. It's a small amount. I knew I could use that money as my initial investment and then pay them back."

"You had no right to steal more money to make up for your father's debt," I snapped.

"I know." She raised her hands in defense. "But I didn't know any other way to pay you back. My dad liquidated all of my assets. I have nothing. He didn't even leave me a cent."

"We've known this for some time."

Her eyes widened as her lips parted. "You did? How?"

"Because we know everything about our employees."

She stepped out of Nicodemus's embrace and moved in front of me. "Dante, please." Ava had her hands in front of her as if that would keep me from snapping her neck. "Just let me finish. I didn't steal anything from your family. I knew I could get the money back for the clients. They wouldn't miss a few pennies from their dividend checks. Some of your clients are the wealthiest men in the world. A few are in the top five on the Forbes richest list."

"That's beside the point," I said with an attitude.

"Dante." She whispered my name like it was a melody falling from her lips. "I got all of your money back. Plus interest. Assuming the current vig is around five percent, I added another two for the inconvenience."

I laughed at her words. "You call this an inconvenience?"

She sighed. "Seven percent is more than fair. I took an extra risk and turned that seven into ten. It's in an offshore account. So, can we call this even?"

I studied her face. Even with dirt on every inch of her skin, she was still gorgeous.

"I also replaced the money I borrowed from the clients," she added when I didn't answer. "I checked the account earlier. If you hadn't thrown me out of your apartment, I was going to tell you everything."

"We're done." Angelo tapped my shoulder. "You've traumatized our girl enough for one night."

"Agreed," Stefan chimed. "You could have fucking killed her, Dante."

I smirked at my brothers. "Only the strong survive in this world."

"Fucking asshole." Stefan shook his head and extended his hand to Ava. "Come here, baby. Let's get you home."

"Stop coddling her." I shifted my gaze to Ava. "Miss Vianello, I'm not done with you."

Brushing the dirt off the front of her pants, she glanced at me. "It wouldn't kill you to be nice to me, Dante. I made over twelve million dollars for your family, not including the money I washed. I break dozens of laws and never complain. I just do my job. Rinse and repeat seven days a week."

Angelo tipped his head back and laughed. "Our little firecracker."

I climbed out of the hole, nostrils flaring. "You better learn how to speak to me with respect."

Angelo snaked his arm around Ava, taking her from Stefan's arms, and rubbed the top of her head with his knuckles. "You did good, little lamb."

"I'm talking to her." I punched Angelo in the arm. "Knock it off, Lo."

Angelo lifted Ava off the ground and carried her toward the car. "We're done for tonight, big bro. Time to go home."

Stefan tapped me on the back. "Give our girl a break. She told us the truth. We can trust her."

"That's debatable," I challenged as we followed Angelo through the woods.

"Dad will be happy she passed the test," Nicodemus commented.

Even if I wouldn't admit it aloud, I was also relieved. So were my brothers. For as much as I wanted to hate her, I liked her. I liked intelligent, talented people. And it didn't hurt that she was sexy and born into our world.

Ava Vianello was one of us now.

The Boardwalk Queen.

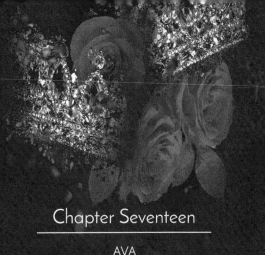

Chapter Seventeen

AVA

A ll the way home, I couldn't stop shaking. Nico held me on his lap and ran his fingers through my hair, whispering sweet things in my ear in Italian. I let him hold me because I needed him. And now, it was becoming abundantly clear how much I missed having him in my life.

After Stefan parked by the loading dock, Nico got out of the SUV and carried me into the building. His brothers didn't follow right away. Instead, they let Nico take me upstairs in the elevator alone. They had traumatized me enough.

Nico brought me straight into my apartment and walked upstairs to the bedroom. He set me on the toilet to turn on the shower and took off his clothes. It was adorable how much Nico cared about me. Even after I told him to get lost, he still hadn't given up on me.

I loved him.

At least, I thought I did.

Until I met Nico, I hadn't felt anything for another man. Nothing more than lust. I cared about Angelo and Stefan, but nothing compared to the butterflies I got in my stomach with Nico.

He dropped each piece of clothing onto the floor, standing before me naked. Then he got on his knees and untied my shoes.

He dropped the dirty sneakers onto the tile and peeled off my sweaty socks. I should have felt self-conscious, smelling like an animal. But with Nico, I didn't care.

So I let him raise my legs, one by one and strip off my yoga pants. I hadn't seen him on his knees since that night on the Ferris wheel. Just thinking about our time together made me wish we could return to that night. To when he wasn't engaged, and things were simpler.

"Nico," I whispered.

His eyes lifted to meet mine.

"I don't want to lose you."

He put his hands on my thighs and leaned forward. "I'm not going anywhere."

Biting my bottom lip, I stared into his eyes, and a single tear slid down my cheek. "I don't want to share you with her. And I know it's not fair to ask you for something I'm not giving you."

"It's okay." He stroked my cheek with his long fingers. "I know you like my brothers. You don't have to choose."

"How can we make this work? Even I don't understand what's happening with all of you." I pushed the hair behind my ears and sighed. "Once upon a time, I was a good girl. And now, I don't even know who I am anymore. Was I always this person?" I rolled my shoulders, hands raised. "I don't know. My dad never let me out of the house. He never let me have friends. I didn't even know what it was like to be normal. I still don't."

"We will protect you better than anyone in this city, Ava." Nico gripped my hips, and with him so close, our lips almost touched. "It's okay to want all of us."

"But Dante hates that I'm with you, Stefan, and Angelo."

He shook his head. "No, he doesn't. He's just mad that he's not getting any from you. Dante likes smart, resourceful people. After tonight, you proved we can trust you. He'll start to see you differently."

Nico lifted me in his arms and carried me into the shower, shutting the glass door behind him. He put me on the tiled floor and backed me beneath the water.

I tilted my head back for Nico to work the shampoo through my hair. "So what now?"

"We want you to be our queen." His fingers massaged my scalp with care. "Even Dante."

"Yeah?"

He bobbed his head. "The kings need a queen. And until now, no woman has ever come close to being worthy of our queen."

"Have you guys shared a lot of women?"

"No, never. Before you, the twins fucked some of the same women. But Dante and me, no."

"Dante doesn't seem like he has sex that often." I laughed. "He's so uptight all the time. Like he's got a pole up his ass."

He snickered. "You're not wrong about that. Dante likes to bear the brunt of the responsibilities so that he can shove them in our faces. He punishes himself because he thinks it makes him better than us."

"I see how much he needs control and order. He's so structured. I've never met anyone who is that disciplined."

After Nico washed the shampoo out of my hair, he started lathering my arms and chest with body wash. It smelled like grapefruit, my favorite. My guys always said I smelled and tasted sweet enough to eat.

"You bring out a different side to him. I've never seen Dante like that with anyone else."

"How so?"

"You're the chaos to his order." Nico bent down in front of me and spread my legs, washing every inch of me. "We're all getting a kick out of how much you push his buttons."

I grabbed his shoulder for support and chuckled. "And I enjoy pushing them."

I couldn't imagine Angelo in the same position without trying to eat my pussy. He only seemed to think of sex when we were together, especially when I was naked. But Nico looked unfazed by my nakedness.

"Nico," I whispered.

He glanced at me, the water dripping in front of his pretty blue eyes. "Yeah, baby?"

"I think I'm falling in love with you."

His hand fell from my body, the brief pause stirring my belly with nerves. He rose from the floor, breathing harder.

"I don't know what love feels like." Cupping my cheek in his big hand, he bent down and kissed my lips. It was quick and left me wanting more. "But I feel something for you, Ava. Maybe it's love."

"This is new for me, too." I hooked my arms around his neck, stood on my tippy toes, and kissed him again. "How do we make this work? You have a fiancee."

"I have a plan." He flashed a wicked grin. "It should get rid of Vittoria."

"Yeah?"

He nodded. "Give me some time. The engagement will be over soon. I'm still not sure why my dad agreed to it."

"To end years of fighting with the Vitales."

"Sure." He shrugged. "But there are other ways we could have gone about it."

"Why do you think your dad is having a change of heart about the Vitales after all these years?"

"Paulie," he said through clenched teeth. "I think he's been in my dad's ear, trying to get him to make moves that make him look weak."

"Why?"

"I don't have any proof. But I think Paulie may be working against the family."

"How does that work with made men?"

"You can't just kill someone because you feel like it," he explained. "The boss has to order the hit. And for someone at Paulie's level, I need evidence to bring to my father. Even with your dad, he didn't want to believe Giancarlo would ever steal from him."

"I was surprised, too. Our parents have been friends their

entire lives. I still can't believe he stole that much money from your family."

He ran his fingers through my hair and nodded. "But you made it up. And in Dante's eyes, that counts for something."

"What will happen to my dad?"

"I don't know yet. But you know how we handle these kinds of things."

I bit my quivering lip. "Yeah, but he's still my dad. Couldn't you exile him? Anything but kill him?"

"We'll cross that bridge when we find him, okay?"

I gulped down my fear. "Okay."

Nico washed and wrapped me in a soft towel. For a man who killed people with his bare hands, he was so damn sweet.

So unexpected.

He lowered me to the bed and got in beside me. Rolling onto his side, he grabbed the back of my head and kissed me like he wanted to devour me. We kissed for a while before he peeled his lips from mine, breathing hard. Dipping his head down, he stuck out his tongue and rolled it over my nipple.

"I missed this," I moaned.

"Me, too," he said before he flicked his tongue over my nipple, then sucked it into his mouth.

I moaned when he pulled my thighs apart, teasing my slit with his finger. "Always so wet for me."

I cried out as he pushed his finger inside me.

"So tight."

He moved between my thighs and added another finger, raising my left leg over his shoulder. And when his tongue rolled over my clit, my skin burst into flames, pricking my skin with tiny bumps. With each kiss he placed on my sensitive skin, he made love to my pussy, devouring me with his tongue.

Moans slipped past my lips, my eyes slamming shut from the waves of pleasure shooting throughout my body. Then Nico's tongue moved inside me, his licks long and aggressive, forcing him to hold down my legs that shook as my orgasm rocked through me.

After I exploded on his tongue, Nico dropped my leg on the bed and licked my juices from his lips. Kissing me hard and fast, he guided his cock to my entrance. I tensed, something I did every time with Nico. He was so big it hurt when he entered me.

"Relax, *passerotta*," he whispered against my lips.

I blew out a deep breath with the first pinch. "I am."

His fingers skated up and down my thigh as he inched into me. "It's okay, baby. I'm not going to hurt you."

"Nico," I whispered as he pushed the rest of the way into me. "Mmm…"

His gentle touch put my body at ease, releasing the tension from my body. But as he moved, and his blue eyes found mine, he stretched me out. However, he was careful not to move too fast. I used to think the Luciano brothers were around the same size. But now I knew that wasn't true.

Because even though the twins were big, I didn't have to adapt so much to them. I didn't feel like my insides were shifting with each thrust.

Lips parted, he brushed my cheek with his fingers. "I missed you, Ava."

Nico kissed me, capturing each of my moans with his mouth. Between kisses, I whispered his name and relaxed beneath him, overcome by the intense ripples of pleasure spreading down my arms. He sucked my lip into his mouth and kissed me like he wanted to drain the air from my lungs.

When his legs trembled, he kissed me again and muttered a few curses in Italian as he came.

"I'm going to do right by you, Ava." Nico raised my hand to his mouth and kissed my skin. "I promise. You'll never have to compete with another woman. I'm sorry I made you feel like you had to."

I curled up on my side and lay my head on his muscular chest.

He ran his fingers up and down my back. "Close your eyes, little sparrow. You need your rest."

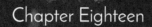

Chapter Eighteen

AVA

Someone knocked on my apartment door. I figured it couldn't have been any of the Luciano brothers. They never bothered to knock before entering my place. My guys barged in here whenever they damn well pleased.

I swung open the door, surprised to find a man in a suit standing in the hallway with a black box with a pink ribbon on the top.

"Miss Vianello," he said with a smile.

"Yes, that's me."

He handed over the box that was so large I had a hard time grabbing it. "Have a good night."

I set the box on the dining room table and tugged on the pink bow. Inside was a strapless black Valentino gown with an invitation on top. After I appraised the dress for a moment, I read the invitation.

You are cordially invited to the Twenty-Fifth Annual Benefactors of the Boardwalk Gala.

The Portofino Hotel and Casino was hosting the event. I wondered which of the brothers had sent me the invitation until I looked at the inner flap of the envelope.

Attendance is not optional.

That fucking asshole.

After he made me dig a grave in the middle of the night and nearly gave me a heart attack, he expected me to attend his stupid party.

Fuck him.

I dropped the note on the table and rushed into the hallway, blowing past two guards on my way to his door.

"Miss Vianello," one man said.

Ignoring him, I balled my hand into a fist and banged on Dante's door.

"Miss Vianello." Another guard moved to my side. "Mr. Luciano is not taking visitors."

"I don't give a damn what Mr. Luciano wants," I fired back as the front door opened.

"You better care," Dante said with venom in his tone.

"How dare you?" I got in his face. "You have some nerve inviting me to your party after what you did to me."

Drinking from the glass in his hand, he surveyed me from beneath his dark brows. "I take it you didn't like the dress I chose for you."

"No, I like it just fine. It's beautiful." I glared at him, nostrils flaring. "You're missing the point, Dante."

He grabbed my wrist and dragged me inside his apartment, slamming the door behind me. "I won't tolerate this kind of behavior, Miss Vianello. Not when you're going to be my date."

"Date?" I scoffed at the idea. "I don't want to be your date. Not after you threw me out of your apartment and made me dig a grave."

"Get over yourself. You sucked my dick. Was I supposed to thank you?" He glanced over his shoulder and smirked. "Or would you rather I pay you?"

"Fuck you! I'm not a whore. I regret ever touching you. It was a mistake."

He clutched my wrists and bent down to speak against my

lips, invading my senses with his masculine scent. A cologne that smelled spicy, mixed with clean linen.

"You forget who you're speaking to." His lips almost brushed mine, and I forgot how to breathe with him so close. "Regardless of what happened, I'm still your boss. So if I say you're my date to the gala this weekend, you will wear the dress and a smile and act the part."

I didn't have much leverage now that my dad was gone. This wasn't the brightest idea, which didn't occur to me until he was breathing in my face. Dante could have killed me with his bare hands. And with him tightening his grip, a tremor of fear rocked through my body.

"I will be your date," I bit out, still feeling somewhat brave, despite the circumstances. "On one condition."

He loosened his grip on my wrists and waited for me to finish my request.

"I want one dance from you."

Dante laughed in my face. "Not a chance."

"That's the only way I'll go with you."

"Bold words for a woman who doesn't have a choice."

I brushed my lips on his. He let go of my wrists and stepped back, looking as if he were sick to his stomach from touching another human being.

"One dance," I said again since he didn't respond. "That's the deal."

Setting his empty glass on the kitchen counter, he looked out the patio doors at the Atlantic Ocean. "Fine, I'll dance with you." His head snapped to me. "But don't push your luck."

I gave him a victorious smile. "I'll see you on Saturday."

He nodded, then refilled his glass with scotch. "Very well."

O n Saturday night, Dante stormed into my apartment without knocking. He dressed in a black tuxedo that molded to his muscular body, paired with a black bowtie. I stood in front of the mirror on the dining room wall and fixed my hair into place, glancing at him in the mirror.

Dante looked good enough to eat.

"Good evening, Mr. Luciano," I said in a snarky tone, giving him a shit-eating grin. "Ever hear of a doorbell?"

"I'll come over here whenever I want." He stuffed his hands into his pockets, his eyes moving over each curve of my body. "Are you done fussing over yourself? I can't be late for my party."

"I wish you would stop taking everything so seriously," I said as he dragged me out of the apartment and headed toward the elevator. "It wouldn't kill you to have fun for once in your life."

When the doors opened, he pushed me inside the empty car. "It might."

On the ground floor, Dante kept his eyes ahead as if he were on a mission. We strolled through the casino, which smelled of smoke. I fanned my hand in front of my face and coughed.

"Did you bring your inhaler with you?"

"It's in here." I raised my purse. "Don't worry. I won't be dying on you tonight."

He pulled open the door, moving his hand to my lower back as he ushered me inside the massive room. At least a hundred people were already here.

Clinging to Dante's side, I moved through the ballroom and smiled. This was all for show. After years of being forced to attend the Lucianos events, I knew what was required.

Laugh on cue.

Smile and be polite.

Don't drink too much.

Never speak out of turn.

My father had coached me through many events over the

years. It was the first time he wasn't here with me. He ran and didn't even care about the consequences for me. I would have been dead if the Luciano brothers hadn't liked me.

People whispered as I passed them. Some offered fake smiles when our gazes met. Were they talking about Dante or me? Or were they gossiping about my father? My skin was seconds from bursting into flames from their heated stares.

I'd never seen Dante with a woman on his arm. So perhaps they were whispering about him and how this was somewhat out of character. And as he made his rounds, I felt like a queen on the arm of a king.

A Boardwalk King.

One day, Dante would take over for his father and become the most important man in Atlantic City. He was already the second most important. Being with him drew a lot of attention to me. Women pursed their lips. Some even shook their heads in disbelief. Men stripped me bare with their eyes.

"That's Ava Vianello," a pretty brunette said with her hand in front of her mouth. "She's beautiful."

I couldn't hear her friend's response because Dante went straight to the bar.

Dante ordered our drinks and then turned to look at me. He dipped his head down and whispered in my ear. "John Zabatino is here." His lips brushed my earlobe. "Turn your head slowly to the right but don't stare."

I did as he instructed and spotted a tall, dark-haired man with a scruffy beard. He was dressed in a black suit, appearing out of place beside men like Dante, who wore tuxedos.

"Did you know he would be here?"

"No one invited him," Dante said in a deep but calm tone. "Fucking bottom feeder. Men like Johnny Z are leeches." Then he moved his hand to my waist, pulling me closer. "Don't leave my side tonight. Do you understand me?"

"Okay," I bit out. "But what if I have to use the bathroom?"

"Then you tell me, and I'll ensure it's safe."

The glass in my hand shook from my nerves. "Why are you acting like he's going to kidnap me?"

His jaw clenched as he let his eyes wander around the room for a moment, trying to act casual. "Because I don't trust him."

I read the truth in his eyes, saw the concern on his face. He was worried about Johnny Z touching me. Even Stefan feared he would find out about me.

"Suddenly so protective for a man who pretends to hate me."

"I don't hate you, Ava." He clutched my chin, those golden-brown eyes searing through me. "If he were to touch you, I'd lose my fucking mind."

Dante snapped his fingers at two armed men in suits. He moved away from the bar and muttered for them to remove John Zabatino from the event. They rushed across the ballroom, and each grabbed one of John's arms.

His gaze went straight to Dante. He struggled to get out of the security guards' grasp, but it was a waste of time. The men were taller and more muscular, forcing him out of the room. Guests stopped talking and tipped up their noses at the commotion.

"That's not going to be the end," I said to Dante. "Is it?"

He shook his head and sipped from his glass. "This is the start of another war."

I extended my hand to Dante, and he looked at it, eyes narrowed. "You promised me one dance."

"Not now." He put his empty glass on the bar and angled his body to scan the room. "I have more important things to worry about at the moment."

I wiggled my fingers in front of his face, not giving up without a fight. "Dance with me, Dante." I flashed a sexy smile. "It will take your mind off things."

"Johnny Z is the least of my problems."

Placing my hand on his chest, I felt his heart beat beneath my fingers and looked into his eyes. "Please, Dante. You promised. And I know you're not a man who backs out of deals."

"Fine," he groaned. "One dance."

He led me onto the dance floor, where at least a dozen couples danced to a slow song. Most of the guests were busy eating and drinking. Some were out on the balcony smoking cigars.

The twins were with their father. Nico was with Vittoria, staring at me from across the room. I hated seeing him with the enemy, but it was part of the show. He had a plan to get rid of her, so I had to trust him.

I hooked my arms around Dante's neck. His hands moved to my waist, but he wasn't aggressive like his brothers.

"This isn't so bad, right?"

"I don't enjoy human contact."

I laughed at his word choice. "You sound like a robot when you say things like that."

He narrowed his eyes at me. "I'm not a robot."

"Then start acting human. Even the way you move is robotic like you're repeating the motions from memory." I pressed my chest to his and breathed in his spicy cologne. "You don't have to be in control all the time, Dante."

"Yes, I do."

"Lose control with me." I breathed on his lips. "I still think about the last time you did when I'm alone at night."

He stared at me as if he were trying to extract the thoughts from my mind. "How often do you think about me?"

"A lot." I licked my lips. "More than I should."

When the song ended, he released me from his grasp and took a few steps back. Our rare moment of intimacy ended as quickly as it began.

"Come." He raised his hand to beckon me. "I'll introduce you to the mayor of Atlantic City. He's interested in investing in the hedge fund."

Just like that, he shifted back to his cold, emotionless self, all business. But it was fun while it lasted.

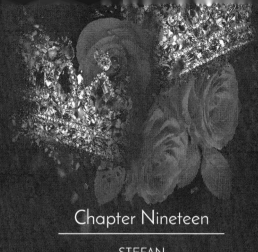

Chapter Nineteen

STEFAN

A va strolled into my office on Sunday night with Tony Natale. He'd started as my driver five years ago and now served as her bodyguard. Tony was good at his job and one of my top guys.

I trusted him with my girl.

Ava swayed her narrow hips, beaming a smile as she hopped onto my lap. I tipped my head at Tony and gestured for him to leave us. I'd been so busy dealing with shit from Johnny Z and his crew all week that I hadn't spent much time with my girl.

I slid my arm behind her back. "I hear you're behaving yourself."

She chuckled. "Who told you that?"

"Dante gives us daily reports about you."

"Of course he does." Ava sucked my bottom lip into her mouth. "I came early so we could spend more time together. I haven't seen you all week. Dante has been a pain in my ass."

I brushed her cheek with my thumb, staring into her eyes. "Bossing people around gives him purpose. You'll get used to it after a while."

"Is that why you and Angelo never talk back to him?"

I shrugged against the leather chair. "Our brother has given up a lot for us. If he needs something, we'll do it. No questions asked."

"Even Nico?"

"Especially Nico. He's been trying to get Dante to like him since we were kids. But he's too dense to realize Dante doesn't like anyone."

"He likes you and Angelo."

"It's different with us. Dante thinks of us as sons, not brothers, because we were so young when our mom died. Nico was in high school and wasn't around that much."

"Why not?"

"Nico lived in the same house as us, but he didn't have the same upbringing. He spent seven years in Manhattan for college. It was just Dante, Angelo, and me for all those years. And even when Nico was in high school, he wasn't home much. He had girlfriends and played sports. We rarely saw him."

"Well, you guys don't treat him like he's your brother. So maybe he stayed away because he didn't feel wanted."

"Alright, that's enough of this heart-to-heart shit for one night." I rose from the chair, bringing her with me. "Have you ever given a lap dance?"

Ava shook her head, dark strands of hair falling into her eyes. "No. Are you going to show me?"

"Nah, I asked one of our best girls to give you a few tips."

"Okay." Her smile lit up her face. "I'll give it a try. But if I suck at it, don't make fun of me."

I opened the door and hooked my arm around her. "Not a chance. And there's no way to mess up a lap dance."

"I'm not a good dancer."

"You don't need to be." I led her down the hallway toward the VIP room. "It's like riding my cock but with a little more of a tease."

"So it's not dancing?"

"Not really. It's seduction. If you can shake your ass and take off clothes, you can give a lap dance."

I tugged on Ava's hand as we entered the second door on our

right. With all of the Johnny Z shit out of the way for the night, I planned to take my sweet ass time with Ava.

Roxy waited for us in front of the bar. She was in her mid-twenties and had reddish-brown hair and big fake tits falling out of a piece of fabric that looked like a bikini top. But it was so thin and small that it served no purpose. And it was see-through.

She sauntered over to us, her tits bouncing, wearing a black G-string.

"Ava, this is Roxy."

Ava extended her hand, but Roxy hugged her instead. "Nice to meet you. The boss talks about you a lot."

"Shut it," I said in a playful tone.

Roxy's eyes landed on me, a smile in place. "Sorry, boss. But women like to hear their men talk about them when they're not around."

Ava nodded, grinning ear to ear as she looked at me. "You talk about me." She blinked a few times. "So cute."

"Enough of that." I pointed my finger at the leather couches on the other side of the mirrored room. "Less talking and more dancing."

Roxy slid her fingers down to Ava's forearm. "Do you want to watch me first or get right to it?"

Ava looked at me. "What do you want?"

"You."

Without a word, Roxy moved behind Ava and placed her hands on her narrow hips. They swayed to the rock song pumping through the speakers.

"A good lap dance is all about the tease," Roxy said to Ava in a seductive tone, running her fingers down her thighs. "By the time the song ends, he should be begging you to sit on his face."

My cock grew harder with each gentle sway of Ava's hips. I couldn't stand another second of not touching her. So I beckoned Ava with my index finger.

Roxy whispered into Ava's ear, and my girl put her palms on my thighs. Her tits were falling out of her top as she danced for me. She licked her lips as our eyes met, following Roxy's orders, moving her body as if she'd done this before.

After torturing me for too long, Roxy told Ava to get on the leather couch with me. Ava straddled my thighs, slowly moving her hands up my chest and shoulders. Roxy sat beside us, her hand on Ava's back. My sweet girl seemed to enjoy being coached, mimicking Roxy's movements.

Ava flicked her tongue over her lip to tease me, rubbing her pussy on my hard cock. I couldn't wait, so I reached into my pocket, pulled out a handful of hundred-dollar bills, and handed them to Roxy. "We're good. You can go back to the stage."

She took the money with a bright smile. "Thanks, boss."

After the door closed behind her, I slid my hands up the backs of Ava's thighs and grabbed her ass. "You're a natural, baby. Fuck, you got me so hard. I need to be inside you."

She hooked her arms around my neck and yelped when I squeezed her ass. "But I'm not done dancing for you."

I pulled down her top, excited when I discovered she wasn't wearing a bra. So I shoved down her tank top, bunching it around her waist. Taking her nipple between my teeth, I tugged hard and watched her eyes slam shut.

A soft moan escaped past her lips.

"Stefan," she whispered. "Mmm… that feels so good."

I dipped my hand beneath her skirt and pushed her panties to the side, testing her slickness with my finger.

She hissed as I touched her.

"Always so wet for me." I inched into her, and her inner walls squeezed my finger. "And so fucking tight."

Ava unzipped my pants and put my dick inside her.

Her pretty lips parted as she took all of me in one quick thrust. "Oh, God. Stefan," she whimpered when she looked at me. "I missed you."

I kissed her lips. "I missed you, too, baby."

Her fingers burrowed into my shoulders as I stretched her out, thrusting deeper. Matching my movements, she moaned against my neck and kissed my skin.

I chose this room because of the mirrored walls. My eyes wandered between my girl and the mirrors, staring at her from every angle.

She was fucking perfect.

I fucked her for close to an hour before she was a sweaty mess, her skin slick. After we both came, our cum dripped onto my pants.

She gasped. "Shit. I'm sorry, Stefan."

"I don't give a fuck. I can get another suit. But I can't replace you."

"Are you saying you're going to keep me?" Ava waggled her eyebrows at me. "That you can't get enough of me?"

"Baby, I'm never letting you go." I kissed her pretty lips. "You're mine."

Outside the room, I heard people shouting. Their voices grew louder as they moved down the hallway toward us. A woman sobbed as someone knocked on the door.

Ava covered her heart with her hand. "What's going on?"

"Who fucking knows?" I patted her knee. "Stay here."

I tucked myself into my pants and rose from the couch to open the door. Tony was on the other side, running a hand through his hair. Candace and Vanessa stood behind him, but his big ass body blocked most of my view. They were crying, mascara streaming down their cheeks.

"Boss, we got a problem." Tony groaned, blowing out a deep breath. "Johnny Z sent our girls back in bad shape."

He tipped his head at the girls. "Look at what he did to Candace and Vanessa."

"Let me get a good look at you two." I raised my hand to beckon them. "Come here. I won't hurt you."

The girls moved in front of Tony, shaking uncontrollably, dressed in ripped clothes with black and blue marks on their face, arms, and chest.

"Jesus." I shook my head. "I'm gonna kill that *pompinaro*."

A few weeks ago, I went to Johnny Z's club and knocked him around until he gave back the girls he stole from us. I paid him back by taking half of the girls from his strip clubs to spite him. We'd been going back and forth for years, our businesses in direct competition with the other.

"This isn't going to stop." Scrubbing a hand across my cheek, I looked at Tony. "We have to get rid of that fucking family."

My father tried to prevent future bloodshed in Atlantic City by forcing Nico to marry Vittoria Vitale. But we weren't the only connected men in this city.

Johnny Z and his crew had been a pain in our families' sides for years. So now that we were coming together, it made sense for us to eliminate them. But my dad was set on bringing peace to AC. He was sick of all the violence and how it impacted our casino.

"Take care of Candace and Vanessa," I said to Tony. "Give them three months' pay. Have someone sit on their houses in case Johnny Z's guys come back for them."

Tony gripped the girl's shoulders and told them to return to the dressing room, where he would meet them. After they walked down the hallway, out of earshot, he said, "What do you want me to do with Johnny Z?"

I glanced over my shoulder at Ava and lowered my voice. "Send Pete and Vinnie to collect Johnny's second in command. Make sure Johnny gets the message not to fuck with the kings."

Tony bobbed his head and walked away.

I locked the door behind him and resumed my place beside Ava, not wanting to alarm her.

"Are we in danger?" Ava clutched my forearm and stared into my eyes as if she were searching for the truth.

"No," I lied, flipping through all the messages on my cell phone. "But you should get going soon. Angelo has been texting me every five minutes. He misses you."

She needed to leave and get as far away from this place as possible for her safety.

Today, it was our girls.

Next week, it could be Ava.

And I couldn't take that risk.

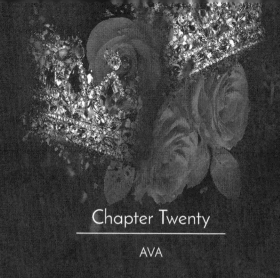

Chapter Twenty

AVA

On the morning of my twenty-second birthday, I woke up to the sound of several voices on the first floor. Bacon and sausage floated through the air, accompanied by several delicious aromas. Nico and Dante both liked to cook. But I doubted Dante was doing anything nice for his captive.

I smiled at the thought of Nico making me breakfast again. He was so sweet and nothing like his brothers. When I was with Nico, I felt loved and seen. Nico gave me a sense of peace, which I needed in this time of confusion and unrest.

My dad was still out there.

They were still looking for him.

I slid my legs off the side of the bed and clutched my chest. My dad was rarely home for my birthdays. After he sent my mom away, I spent most days with the staff. Enzo and Angelina were more like my parents.

At least I would see them tonight.

My dad would be another no-show.

I climbed out of bed and tied a silky black robe around my waist. After brushing my hair and teeth, I padded toward the stairs in a pair of fuzzy slippers.

I stood at the top of the stairs and watched all four of them. They were all so gorgeous… and mine. To my surprise, Dante and Nico were in front of the stove. Dante wore an apron with his usual black designer suit beneath it.

I smiled so hard my cheeks hurt.

Nico wore a suit with a Kiss the Chef apron around his neck. For a split second, I couldn't help but wonder what the two of them would look like in nothing but the aprons.

"Nicodemus, move out of my way." Dante tapped his brother with his elbow. "I'm trying to cook."

"So am I."

"Why are you two fighting over cooking?" Angelo propped himself up on his elbows at the kitchen island, sitting beside his twin. "Can you do anything together without getting into a pissing match?"

"No." Stefan laughed. "They'd kill each other first."

"It's my birthday," I said on my way down the stairs, "and it would be nice if all of you could get along for a few hours."

All four heads snapped to me.

Nico dropped a spatula on the counter and rushed over to greet me. He swept me into his arms and kissed me. "Happy birthday, *mi amore.*"

I smiled in response and kissed him again. But it didn't last long because Stefan pulled me away from Nico and crushed my lips with a kiss.

His fingers traced the length of my jaw, a smile on his handsome face. "Happy birthday, *bellezza.* I got you something special to wear for tonight."

Before I could respond, Angelo stole me away from his twin and lifted me off my feet, carrying me into the kitchen. "I got you something money can't buy." He kissed my lips as he set me on the kitchen island and moved between my thighs. "Happy birthday, *dolcezza.* It's going to be a night you never forget."

I raised a curious eyebrow at him. "Oh, yeah?"

He nodded.

"So, what did you get me?"

"You'll see." He fisted my hair, parting my lips with his tongue. "I haven't shown you each room at the club."

I grinned with delight. "So it's that kind of surprise?"

Stefan moved to my side and gripped my leg. "We'll all be there." His fingers inched up my inner thigh. "You'll like it."

I glanced over at the stove. "Even Dante?"

"Yes," Dante said as he approached us. "Even me."

I wet my lips with my tongue as our eyes met. "And what did you get me?"

"Is cooking your breakfast not enough?"

"I know what I want from you."

He pushed his brothers out of the way and took Angelo's place between my legs, putting his palms on both sides of the counter. Dante caged me with his body, and his chest pressed to mine. Our lips were so close that I could feel his breath on my skin.

"What do you want?"

I leaned forward. "I want you to kiss me."

"Ooh, this I wanna see," Angelo said with laughter in his tone.

Dante stepped back, creating some distance between us, still keeping his gaze on me. "Why is a kiss so important to you?"

"Because I want to feel closer to you."

"I don't like intimacy."

"You let me kiss your dick." I gave him a wicked grin that lit up my face. "That counts as touching."

"That's not the same."

Nico returned to the stove to remove the bacon from the frying pan. With Dante distracted, Nico took control of the kitchen and added the batter to the waffle iron.

I spread my thighs and pushed up the robe, so Dante could see I wasn't wearing panties. "You could kiss me here." I dragged my finger down my slit, and he looked like he stopped breathing. "I don't care where you kiss me. But I want a kiss."

"I volunteer," Stefan chimed. "Spread those legs nice and wide for me, baby."

"Me, too," Angelo said from behind me, pulling me backward so he could kiss my lips. "I love eating your pussy."

My eyes drifted back to Dante. "But I want your brother to kiss me first."

Angelo groaned. "He's not going to do it. I'll lick your pussy until you come."

"You want a kiss?" Dante asked to regain my attention, and my focus shifted back to him. He raised his hand and beckoned me with his finger. "Come here."

I sat up and leaned forward, resting my palms on my thighs. "No, you come to me. It's my birthday."

He resumed his place between my legs and shook his head. "You're such a little brat."

"Then punish me."

Gripping my chin, he rubbed the pad of his thumb across my bottom lip. His golden-brown eyes held mine as he breathed through his nose.

I slid my hands up his chest and draped my arms around his neck. "Kiss me, Dante."

His brothers didn't have a problem with intimacy. So his issues couldn't have come from a shared trauma, which made me even more curious about his past.

Why did he only fuck whores?

Why hadn't he kissed a woman?

I had so many questions about Dante. He wasn't as forthcoming as his brothers. And even when I asked them why Dante was like this, they weren't sure. His mother's death was traumatic. And according to Nico and the twins, he hadn't been the same since.

That had to be the source.

"Kiss me." I reached out to grab Dante's hand, and he recoiled from my touch. "Please."

Everyone stopped moving, solely focused on us. Dante looked at each of his brothers, then bent his head down, his lips inches from mine. I couldn't believe he was going to kiss me. For so long, I had wanted to feel something with him. Maybe he just needed to see that he could trust me.

A crooked grin tugged at the corners of his mouth right

before his mouth descended upon mine. He gave me a tentative kiss, and I opened up for him, so his tongue brushed mine.

Dante was initially hesitant, and I could feel the inner war he was fighting with himself. He didn't want to like me. And he didn't want to enjoy kissing me.

But he did.

Because as we kissed, we shed all of our frustration, unleashing a hunger inside both of us. We kissed like we were fighting for possession over the other. Like we wanted to tear each other apart.

I wrapped my legs around his back, and he devoured me like a savage, his hard cock poking me. He was ravenous, consumed by me from the second he lowered his guard. I was so thankful his brothers didn't make any stupid comments.

They didn't even make a sound.

When I moaned into Dante's mouth, he held me down, kissing me so hard my back hit the marble. The kiss was sensual and raw, filled with pent-up desire.

He peeled his lips from mine, his chest rising and falling with each breath. "Happy birthday, Ava."

My eyes widened at the use of my name, and I couldn't stop myself from smiling. It was the first time he hadn't called me Miss Vianello.

Dante was coming around.

I licked my lips, and his eyes followed. "Thank you."

Angelo moved beside his older brother and smirked. "How did it feel to pop your cherry?"

Stefan laughed. "Kissing virgin."

Dante snarled. "Both of you, shut the fuck up."

"Big bro is sensitive," Stefan teased.

"No, I'm not," Dante snapped. "You're idiots." Ignoring the twins' laughter, Dante stepped out from between my thighs and extended his hand. "It's time to eat, good girl."

After we ate breakfast, the five of us sat in the living room. Several boxes were stacked on the coffee table, all wrapped in pretty paper.

Dante handed me a small box with a ribbon on top. Inside was a platinum bracelet with poker chips and playing card charms.

"Dante." I glanced up at him, my mouth hanging open. "Aww, this is so sweet."

He groaned. "Stop that."

"No, I'm soaking up this moment." I rose from the couch and held out the box, gesturing for him to put the bracelet on my wrist. "So thoughtful. I love it."

Dante latched the clasp, securing the bracelet into place, and then I hugged him. He stood there, frozen for a moment, before he hugged me back.

I kissed his cheek. "It's perfect. Thank you."

"Open mine." Stefan shoved a big box into my hands and sat on the couch beside me. "Happy birthday, Ava."

I flipped open the lid and gasped at the black leather Bottega Veneta handbag, unable to stop smiling as I hugged him. "Thank you. But you guys are spoiling me too much."

This bag cost a small fortune.

Dante's bracelet was custom.

I couldn't even imagine what Nico and Angelo had in their boxes. But I was excited to find out.

"It's not too much for you," Stefan said before he kissed me. "I saw you eyeing up this bag."

I smiled. "Thank you, Stefan. Always so perceptive."

"I notice everything about you."

"Okay, you sappy fucker," Angelo cut in as he made room for himself on my right. "Enough of that cheesy shit."

"Fuck you," Stefan snapped at his twin. "Like you don't pay attention to our girl."

Angelo dropped a box into my lap with a wicked grin. "Mine isn't as flashy as these two showoffs." He put his hand on my thigh. "But you'll get much more use out of my present."

"Hmm..." I peeled back the wrapping paper. "If I know you as well as I think I do, this is something sexual."

Angelo's golden brown eyes flickered with deception. "You'll see."

"I was right," I said as I opened the box filled with sex toys.

Dante groaned, shaking his head. "Real classy, Lo."

His shoulders raised a few inches. "Learn to live a little, you stiff fuck." Then he pinned my back to the couch and lifted a vibrator from the box. "We're taking you to The Monella Club later. It's time to break you in."

Shaking my head, I smiled. "You're such a freak."

Angelo sucked my bottom lip into his mouth. "You haven't seen freaky yet."

Nico leaned over the back of the couch and pushed Angelo off me. "It's my turn. Save that shit for later." He set a small box on my lap. "Happy birthday, *passerotta*."

I squealed when I opened the box and found a platinum sparrow dangling from a necklace. The charm was encrusted with diamonds that sparkled. "Nico, this is so sweet. Thank you."

I kissed his lips, and he palmed the back of my head, stealing the air from my lungs.

"My little sparrow," he whispered, stroking the side of my face. He took the necklace from the box and draped it around my neck.

I lifted the charm and smiled. "It's so pretty."

Nico kissed my cheek. "Pretty things for a pretty woman."

"What time are we going to the club?" I looked at each of them. "Because I promised Enzo and Angelina I would come home for dinner. Knowing Enzo, he's preparing a five-course meal and made a three-tier birthday cake."

"Not until closer to midnight," Angelo said. "We have some shit to take care of with Johnny Z's crew."

"Oh, he's still giving you guys trouble?"

They grunted or nodded to confirm.

"Okay, well, go deal with him. I have to shower and get ready for my party."

Each of them kissed me goodbye, wishing me happy birthday again, and then they left my apartment.

Chapter Twenty-One

AVA

A few hours after the guys left my apartment, I sat on the kitchen island stuffing my face with the cupcakes Nico made.

He was so damn sweet.

I licked the icing from the cake. It was sad how many birthdays I spent alone.

Just like this one.

So when I heard the front door close, I didn't expect to see Dante strolling into the living room with a purpose. His eyes stripped me bare, like lasers searing my flesh. He took the cupcake from my hand and threw it into the sink.

"Dante, what are you doing? I was eating that."

He lifted me over his shoulder and smacked my ass. "You can eat all the cupcakes you want later."

As he ascended the stairs, my heart raced. "What are you doing?"

He threw me onto the bed and stripped off his jacket and tie. "I'm going to fuck you." He dropped his shirt onto the floor. "Take off the robe and spread your legs for me."

I disposed of the robe and sat back on my elbows, watching him undress. His eyes moved from my pussy to my face. And after he was completely naked, I sat up and reached out for him.

He swatted at my hand. "No."

I tried to touch his chest as he pushed me onto my back and moved between my thighs. Yet again, he shoved my hand away.

"No touching."

Unlike his brothers, he didn't have a single tattoo. His chest was smooth and tanned, and I was dying to feel his skin pressed against mine. But he wouldn't let me.

Asshole.

"But I want to touch you."

He put one knee between my legs and stroked his long, hard cock. "You begged me to fuck you for the past two months. Do you still want that?"

I bobbed my head. "Yes. Fuck me."

"Then you follow my rules. Understand?"

I cleared my throat. "Okay."

He smirked. "Good girl."

I knew he wouldn't be gentle. So when he thrust into me, filling me to the hilt without letting me adjust to his size, I expected the pain.

"Dante," I moaned, choking on my words as he slammed into me even harder than before.

"Fuck," he hissed, driving into me like a wild animal, showing no signs of slowing down. "Your pussy is so tight. Goddamn it."

His head dropped for a moment, but his pace never faltered. He looked like he was trying hard to focus on anything other than how good this felt.

I was surprised he didn't flip me onto my stomach and take me from behind. His brothers had told me stories about how he only fucked women that way. Because he didn't want to look at them. And God forbid a woman touched him. He probably would have lost his shit.

So I dared to touch him again.

He grabbed my wrists and held them above my head. "What did I tell you?"

"You're inside me. Why can't I touch you?"

Annoyed, he shook his head and lifted his tie from the bed. Fucking me without mercy, he focused on binding my wrists together while he went deeper and deeper, taking me to the brink of madness.

A smirk tugged at the corner of his mouth. Then he raised my bound arms above my head and attached his tie to the headboard.

Like a savage, he pumped into me harder and raised my right leg in the air to change the angle. I loved how he could touch me anywhere he wanted, but I got punished for trying to put my hand on his chest. Not like it mattered. This was the kind of punishment I'd begged him for and only imagined in my dirty dreams.

Eventually, he had both of my legs draped over his shoulders as he fucked me so hard I thought he would leave an indent of his dick inside me.

Thankfully, it was a silk tie, so when it rubbed my skin, it didn't hurt as much. But when Dante rocked his hips, he held me down, getting rougher with each thrust. But I couldn't get enough of him.

Mean.

Rough.

Angry.

I would take Dante Luciano any way I could get him. The darkness inside him called to me.

The headboard banged the wall, hitting it so hard I thought we would crash through it. That didn't slow him down one bit.

His long fingers wrapped around my throat, and his lips parted as if he were so close. I saw the same look from him not that long ago. When I had his big dick in my mouth, he had the same look of pleasure.

I squeezed my legs around him.

His eyes snapped open. "What did I tell you?"

"You're mine, Dante. And I'm yours. So you better get used to me touching you."

That only poked the dragon.

With Dante, I didn't expect him to make love to me. And I didn't expect him to be sweet. So when he unleashed his darkness on me, I screamed his name and begged for more.

I liked when he lost control and gave in to his desire for me. He was rough, branding every inch of my skin with his hands. And when I came again, my body was numb from the pain.

But it felt good.

Like I was high on him.

"You gonna cum again for me, my little slut?" Dante fucked me like he was possessed, going harder and deeper with each thrust.

"Yes," I choked out, my eyes snapping shut from the overwhelming sensations shooting through my body. "I'm coming..."

A wild look danced across his face. "You can still be my good girl." His teeth sank into my thigh. "But I'm going to mark every inch of your body first."

After I came again, I was so sensitive chills rushed down my spine. Every inch of my skin was on fire, tingling from the insane orgasms Dante delivered one after the other.

He bit my other thigh, so I had teeth marks on my skin. I thought Angelo was the one with mental issues. But Bossman was the real lunatic of this family.

Although, he hid it so well.

Dante leaned forward, holding my legs against his chest, his cock sliding so far into me I could feel him everywhere. He invaded my body like he was conquering me, claiming his property.

I screamed.

He growled.

It was perfection.

He owned me.

Ruled me.

Destroyed me.

The headboard hit the wall with a whack. One after the other until the screws must have loosened. Or maybe something snapped. I heard a cracking sound, and the mattress slid off the frame, crashing to the floor with the headboard.

"Dante," I yelled.

He laughed and kept going. It was the first time I'd ever seen what could pass as a smile on his lips.

Man, he was sick.

I stared at him, my eyes wide. "Dante."

He covered my mouth with his hand. "Shhh, I'm not done fucking you."

His hands wrapped around my throat, his thumb sliding over my windpipe. Dante had killed men with his bare hands. He knew how much pressure and where to apply it.

And when he came, his legs shook mine, and he made the sexiest sounds I'd ever heard from a man. He stilled on top of me for a moment, eyes closed as he released his grip on my throat so I could breathe again.

I blew out a few deep breaths to gather myself. "Dante, can you untie me?"

His eyes snapped open to meet mine, still breathing hard. Without a word, he reached forward and worked on freeing my wrists.

I massaged my skin to help with the burning sensation.

Dante pulled out of me, his eyes lowering to the space between us on the mattress. I could feel our cum sliding under my ass.

He looked at my pussy, then at me. I couldn't tell what he was thinking.

Dante was so hard to read.

He got off the bed, went into the bathroom, and returned with a washcloth in his hand. Then he kneeled between my legs and cleaned me up. Unlike his fucking, he was gentle this time. And I was thankful for that because I was sore. There wasn't a single part of me that didn't hurt.

He dabbed at my skin with the washcloth. "I'm not used to fucking girls like you."

"What kind of girls do you fuck?"

"Whores."

He sat at the edge of the bed and didn't push me away when I ran my fingers down his chest.

"I let you treat me like a whore. But we both know I'm not." I sucked on his earlobe. "Don't leave me here with this broken bed, not after you destroyed my pussy."

To my surprise, he wrapped a sheet around my naked body and set my feet on the floor, so he could quickly dress. He yanked my hand, leading me out of the bedroom.

"Where are we going?"

"To my apartment."

Dante carried me downstairs and over to his place, climbing the stairs to his bedroom without a word. I had a feeling this wasn't something he'd ever done before. His bedroom was dark, the bed decorated with black sheets. There wasn't an ounce of color.

He removed his clothes.

I prayed he wasn't ready to have sex again. My body needed more time to heal. His teeth marked my thighs, and his fingers branded every inch of my arms, chest, and neck. There wasn't a single part of me left untouched by this monster.

He headed into the ensuite bathroom without a word, so I sat on his bed. After he came out, he stood in front of me with his hand extended.

I took his hand and leaned in for a kiss, but I didn't get one. "Aren't you going to kiss me?"

He snorted. "No."

"I think I deserve a kiss after you murdered my pussy and wrecked my bedroom."

Dante reached between us and cupped my sex. "Does your pussy hurt?"

I nodded.

"What do you want me to do about it?"

"Kiss me." Our lips were inches apart. "That's one way of apologizing."

"Oh, now I need to apologize for fucking you so good you had four orgasms? Most women would thank me."

"Well, I'm not most women. And I want a kiss."

He rolled his eyes and groaned. "Fine, kiss me."

"Why don't you like kissing?"

"I don't know. Never really thought much about it."

"Haven't you ever wanted to kiss a woman you had sex with?"

Dante shook his head. "Whores don't kiss."

"So you never had a girlfriend?"

"No."

"Why not?"

Dante scrubbed a hand across his jaw. "Because women who get too close to me die."

His mother.

"I'm close to you right now." My lips brushed his. "And I'm not going anywhere."

"No one will ever know about you. It's the only way we can protect you."

"Protect me from who? The Vitales."

"We have a lot of enemies."

"You can touch me without being afraid I'm going to disappear. And I want to touch you, Dante. I have waited so long for this."

He carried me into the bathroom, setting my feet on the floor in front of the garden tub. "You need a bath before you leave for the party."

"I'm not going anywhere until you kiss me."

He smirked. "Fuck, you're annoying."

Then he palmed the back of my head and sucked my bottom lip into his mouth. He bit and pulled until I moaned for him, and after a while, our tongues tangled. Each kiss was angry and hot and unlike any other kiss.

"Get in the tub." Dante smacked my ass. "I'll make your pussy feel better."

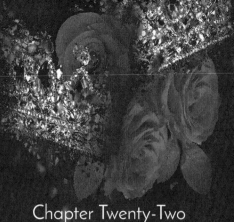

Chapter Twenty-Two

NICO

Giancarlo finally called Ava. It was eight o'clock on the night of her birthday. And as expected, he called to wish her a happy birthday.

I listened to the conversation that confirmed he fucked over our family. As we discussed, Ava got him to tell her every detail. I knew from the start she was on our side and that she would choose us.

I stuffed the phone into my pocket and went straight to Dante's penthouse. If it were a typical night, he would have eaten dinner at seven and returned to work. But the four of us had planned to take Ava to The Monella Club. Angelo had a few ideas to push Ava out of her comfort zone.

And now that we had a lead on Giancarlo, the club could wait for another night. I balled my hand into a fist and banged on Dante's door.

He opened after the second knock.

"Giancarlo called Ava." I held up my cell phone. "I recorded the call."

With that, he held the door and gestured for me to enter his apartment. I strolled down the long white-and-black marble hallway and followed him to the living room. The space had little personality, but I wasn't one to talk. I never even bothered to decorate my apartment—just a few things here and there added by the interior decorator.

"Giancarlo told Ava how to access the money."

Dante sat in the oversized leather armchair and extended his hand for me to sit on the couch. "What did he say?"

I let him listen to the audio, then sent a copy of the transcription to his phone.

He tipped his head at me, then drank from a glass of scotch. "You did good, Nico."

Nico, not Nicodemus.

Now that we were sharing a woman, he was coming around, treating me more like his equal. About fucking time. It only took twenty-five years and one feisty woman to bring us together.

After Dante let the recording play twice, he hopped off the couch, jaw clenched.

"We're going over to the Vianellos house. We need access to Giancarlo's safe," Dante said on our way out of his apartment. "Ava can open it." He tapped the button on the wall and waited until we were inside the elevator before saying, "Call Stefan and Angelo. Get them over to Ava's house. We do this together."

Chapter Twenty-Three

AVA

H*appy birthday to me.*

Except it wasn't all that happy, another day spent with the staff, who were only here because my father paid them. Dad confessed to his crimes before dinner, as my guys had hoped. Nico admitted to listening to my phone calls and reading my texts and emails.

I wasn't mad.

From the start, I assumed they were tracking my every movement. That was the reason I never spoke about business over the phone. I never even mentioned it to Bella in our daily chats.

I sat at the head of the table in the main dining room. Tears pricked my eyes, so desperately wanting to fall. But I slapped on a happy face. Even though my guys weren't going to kill me, they would probably whack my dad. That was how they handled business.

Dad was a coward.

I knew he would run.

The bastard fucked me over, stole my money, and left me here to rot. Not much of a surprise. He only did shit that suited him.

"Happy birthday, Ava, happy birthday to you," Enzo and Angelina finished singing in unison with the staff.

The three-tiered cake was more appropriate for a wedding, not my twenty-second birthday. It was a sweet gesture. But as I stared at the monstrosity before me, my chest ached from losing my parents. Angelina was on my right, Enzo on my left. They were the only people who kept me going when I was home. A handful of staff crowded around the table. They clapped and wished me a happy birthday.

Enzo smacked a kiss on my cheek. "Happy birthday, Ava."

Angelina kissed my other cheek and whispered, *"Buon compleanno, mi amore,"* in my ear, which translated to happy birthday, my love in Italian.

I kissed her back. "Thanks, Ang."

"How about some champagne to celebrate?"

After we drank and ate cake, I got up from the table and went into the kitchen. I swiped a water bottle from the refrigerator, and Enzo was standing across from me when I spun around.

"You're upset," he said.

I forced a smile for his benefit. "It's nothing."

He inched closer, a warm smile on his face. "I know you miss your parents." Enzo extended his arm toward the living room. "Your father left presents for you to open. How about we do that next?"

Before I could answer him, a loud bang echoed. A shiver ran down my arms. It sounded like it came from the front of the house.

Enzo hooked his arm around me and opened the pantry door. "There's a secret entrance." He moved a few boxes of pasta out of the way and then hit a small latch.

He pushed on the wooden shelf, which swung into the wall, exposing a secret passage. We'd lived in this house for over two decades, and I had never known about this hidden door.

Gunshots sounded, one after the other.

Enzo tapped my back. "Get in."

"Where does this lead?" I choked out, my voice trembling with each word I spoke.

Enzo removed a gun from the waistband of his pants. "To the wine cellar."

Since when does he carry a weapon?

And what kind of chef needs a gun?

"Hide in the wine cellar. I have to round up the staff. We'll meet you downstairs." His palm tapped my back with more force. "Go. Now. There's no time to waste, Ava."

I took one last look at Enzo and stepped into the dark passageway.

Enzo locked the door behind me.

Sucking in a deep breath, I put my hand over my heart to calm myself. It was dark and cold, with nothing but the sound of my heart beating loudly in the small space. I breathed through my nose, doing my best to control my anxiety. My inhaler was in my purse in the living room.

You can do this.

I crept down the narrow staircase, nearly tripping over my feet. The cold, stone wall broke my fall. My heart beat faster, the thumping louder in my ears as I inched my way down the stairs with caution.

Once my feet hit the ground floor, I expelled the air from my lungs. The motion-detecting lights on the walls illuminated as I walked toward the back of the house.

I heard footsteps slap the concrete floor.

Glancing over my shoulder, I spotted a man dressed in a suit. He wasn't Enzo or any of the staff. My heart raced into overdrive from the adrenaline shooting through my veins.

Shoving down my fear, I bolted down the corridor. I could smell the grapes as I ran into the wine cellar, searching for a weapon—anything to help me subdue my attacker. So I fisted a wine bottle opener and hid behind a barricade of casks stacked up to the ceiling.

"Come out, come out, little girl," the man taunted as he moved closer. "I just want to talk."

Yeah, right.

I gripped the bottle opener so hard it dug into my palm.

Sweat dripped down my back, and my entire body felt like it was on fire.

The man stood in the entryway to the room. Peeking out from behind a cask, I watched him move across the right side. I crawled toward the exit, careful not to make a sound. But I dropped the bottle opener, which scraped the floor.

"Come out," he taunted in a harsh tone. "I won't hurt you."

He was hovering over me within seconds, staring at me from between two stacks of casks.

I attempted to run.

But he hooked his big arm around me, cutting off my air supply as his large hand closed over my windpipe. "Where is your father hiding?" Then he reached into his pocket and showed me a knife. "Tell me. Now!" The blade grazed the tops of my breasts but didn't go deep enough to leave a mark. "Or I will cut the answer out of you."

Before he could slice into my skin, a figure appeared at the entrance to the wine cellar. "Get your fucking hands off her."

Nico aimed a gun at his head.

The man laughed. "Her father owes us a lot of money. You know how this works, Nicodemus. The girl has to pay for his sins."

Thanks, Dad.

Asshole.

Teeth gritted, Nico shot the man in the head without a second thought. His blood splattered on my face and clothes. The man dropped to the floor beside me.

I raised my hands to wipe my face and screamed at the sight of so much blood on me. Without a second to process anything, Nico scooped me into his arms and carried me out of the wine cellar.

On our way to the pantry entrance, he tucked the hair behind my ear. "This isn't the birthday you wanted. But we'll make it up to you."

Chapter Twenty-Four

DANTE

I shot the last assassin in the head, his blood splattering on the wall. He dropped to the floor like a sack of potatoes by Angelos' feet. So my brother kicked him in the head a few times to make sure he was dead.

"Dickhead," he said with another kick, getting blood on his black Ferragamo.

If I hadn't already wanted to whack Giancarlo before tonight, I did now. His recklessness could have gotten Ava killed. These men were sent here to bring her back to the Vitales as payment for his debts.

Nicodemus brought Ava upstairs with blood on her face and clothes, trembling with her arms wrapped around his neck. She sobbed on his shoulder, her eyes aimed at me. They were red-rimmed and glassy.

I stepped in front of them and shoved the gun into the holster. "What happened?"

"I killed Dominic Rossi." Nicodemus set Ava's feet on the floor in the kitchen, holding her against his chest. "He came here looking for the money Giancarlo owes him. Good thing we got here in time, or he would've taken Ava."

I narrowed my eyes at Ava. "How much money does your father owe?"

She bit her bottom lip, unable to meet my gaze. "My dad took a loan from the Vitales to pay back what he stole from you. I'm not sure how much. He never said."

My nostrils flared at her confession. "And he was still short ten million?"

Ava nodded. "Not including the seven million he stole from me." She shifted her weight from one foot to the other. "He said he lost a lot of money to new investments."

We got our money back from Ava, but only because our girl was a fucking genius.

"Nico overheard your phone call with your dad." I clutched her shoulder and steered her down the hallway. "Show us to your father's office. We heard what he said about the money."

Ava led the way to Giancarlo's office. It was the size of a living room with a large oak desk at the center and built-in bookshelves.

"My dad keeps everything in the safe." She walked toward a Monet painting hung on the interior wall. "I'm not sure what's in here. But maybe it will help us figure out where he went."

Our captive had resigned to the fact her father fucked her over and left her to die. But luckily for Ava, she was one of us now. We would protect her from our enemies and her father's. Proving her loyalty to my family changed how I felt about her.

We could trust her.

Angelo pulled the painting off the wall, so Ava could enter her father's passcode into the safe. The door clicked open, and she stepped aside for me to look inside.

Not surprisingly, there wasn't any cash or checks. Just a list of foreign bank account numbers with the PINs and authorization codes.

I lifted a gold key and showed it to Ava. "Do you know what this goes to?"

"A safe deposit box at a local bank."

I pocketed the key. "Do you know what he keeps there?"

"My dad said he had fake credentials made for me, so I could run."

"What else did he say?"

"He told me to buy a one-way plane ticket to the Bahamas."

Angelo moved beside me, hands shoved into his pockets. "So that's where he went. But how? Our guys didn't find any record of Giancarlo leaving the country."

"He must have friends we don't know about."

With her top lip quivering, she stood in front of me. "Please don't kill him. I'll do anything you want. Just let my dad live."

"You know I can't do that," I fired back. "If I make an exception for one person, then others will think they can steal from us and get away with it."

"But I paid you back plus interest." She shoved her palms into my chest, sobbing. "Dante, please. Let him go. He won't come back."

I clutched her wrists, teeth gritted. "This is how we do business."

"Please," she choked out, tears streaming down her cheeks.

A strange sensation tore through my chest. This girl was growing on me, and I couldn't stay away despite how much I fought my desire for her.

I had to have her.

"Dante, c'mon." Angelo rested his hand on my shoulder. "We can make an exception for Ava. She's right. Giancarlo won't come back here. And she settled his debts."

Ava swiped at the tears staining her cheeks and then threw herself into Stefan's arms.

"Did the bad man hurt you?" Stefan joked with his eyes on me. "My brother is mean. But he likes you. Dante refuses to admit it."

"Shut up."

Stefan dabbed at the blood and tears on Ava's cheeks with his shirt. "No more crying, baby. It's your birthday. Cheer up."

I moved past them and lifted a folded slip of paper.

It was Ava's birth certificate.

I showed it to Nicodemus.

His eyebrows rose. "That's interesting."

156

"Very." I bobbed my head. "I wonder if this is true."

"Only one way to find out," he said in a hushed tone, careful not to attract Ava's attention to us. "I'll grab Giancarlo's toothbrush from the bathroom."

"Get as many samples as you can. We need proof before we show this to Dad."

I tucked Ava's birth certificate into the inner pocket of my suit jacket. There was no way she knew the truth. Because if she had, I doubted she would have tried to protect Giancarlo.

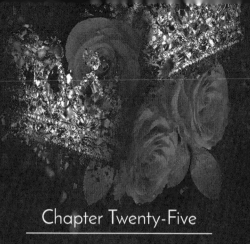

Chapter Twenty-Five

NICO

I was in the middle of mixing waffle batter when Ava stumbled downstairs, her dark hair hanging over her shoulders. She scrubbed a hand at her eyes and yawned. "Are you making me waffles?"

Ava was my weakness.

My addiction.

I pointed at the stool in front of the kitchen island. "Sit."

Like a good girl, she followed orders. I poured the batter over the waffle iron and closed the lid with my back to her. Even from a distance, she smelled intoxicating. A fruity scent that always lifted off her skin.

I poured her a glass of orange juice and set it on the counter in front of her.

"What's going to happen with the Vitales?" She sipped her juice, watching me from beneath her dark brows. "Will they come for me?"

I shook my head. "No, you're untouchable."

Only because I made a plan with my brothers last night after we brought Ava home. None of us wanted to marry into the Vitale family. And since Vittoria would arrive within the hour, I knew one way to get her to call off the wedding.

I had to break her fidelity rule.

"Remember when I said I want a dirty little slut who will get on her knees for me in the bedroom?" I moved between her spread thighs and pulled down her lip with my thumb. "Let me do anything I want. I want to fuck you like a whore."

She giggled, and it was cute.

Our girl was inexperienced and naive, but we slowly broke her in.

"I know you've been holding out on me, Nico." Ava peeked up at me, tucking her lip between her teeth. "I'm not a good girl anymore."

"What did I tell you about biting that lip?" I hooked my tie around her neck and pulled her to me, squeezing hard enough for her to gasp.

"Maybe you should do something about it, Nicodemus."

I growled against her mouth. "You want to play games with me, *puttana*."

She wrapped her legs around my back. "*Vaffanculo, bastardo*," she shot back with laughter in her voice.

"*Troia*," I said before I parted her lips with my tongue.

She was my little slut.

Mine.

I lifted her onto the counter and stripped off her shorts and panties. She sat with her palms on the marble and spread her thighs, leaning back on her elbows. "Look how wet I get for the bastard of the family." Ava traced her finger up her slit and smirked. "You should see how hot I get for Dante."

I choked her with my tie, shoving down my pants and boxer briefs. I didn't even give her a second to adjust before I slammed into her.

Fuck, she felt like heaven.

I buried myself so deep inside her that she screamed. "Take my cock, little whore."

Her head fell back, black hair spilling behind her. "Nico," she moaned. "I'm coming."

"No. You don't get to cum."

I pulled out as her body started convulsing, punishing her for

159

calling me a bastard. I flipped her onto her stomach and smashed her cheek into the black marble, tightening my grip on the tie with the other hand.

"Do you like fucking my brothers?" She moaned in response, and I slapped her ass hard. "Act like a whore, and I'll treat you like one."

Smoke filled the kitchen from the waffle iron.

Fuck.

What was with us and waffles? The same shit happened when I kissed her for the first time.

"Don't move."

I dumped the burnt waffles into the sink, unplugged the appliance from the wall, and turned on the exhaust fan before the smoke alarm went off.

I moved behind her and leaned forward to taste her, splitting her open with my tongue. This wasn't how I would treat a whore.

But I needed a taste.

Ava writhed beneath me as I held her down with my palm on her back. "Shhh, baby. If you make a sound, I won't let you come."

"Nico," she groaned. "Stop torturing me."

"Only good girls get to come." I spanked her ass. "You're a bad girl, remember? Or do I need to remind you?"

I lifted her off the island and put her bare feet on the tiled floor. "Stay there." I removed the rest of my clothes. "Take off your shirt."

She pulled the silky spaghetti strap top over her head and threw it onto the floor.

"Good girl." I patted my palm on my thigh. "Now crawl to me."

Her eyes widened.

I tapped my leg again and smirked. "Obey your master, *puttana.*"

She got on her knees and winced. The tile was cold and hard, but she did as instructed. My tie hung loosely around her neck, taunting me to choke her again. By the time I finished, I would mark every inch of her skin.

That sexy ass.

Her perfect tits.

Every part of her.

My good girl.

Ava stared up at me, on her knees, waiting for me to tell her what to do next. She wanted to come so bad she would have done anything.

I fisted my shaft and tipped my head. "Suck my cock."

Ava wrapped her hand around me and took half of me into her mouth. I laid my hand on her head and forced more of me down her throat. She gagged, and I rocked my hips.

Tears leaked from her eyes and streamed down her cheeks. I wiped them away and moved back, so my cock popped out of her mouth.

Running the pad of my thumb across her lip, I winked. "Good girl."

She smiled.

I got on my knees and flipped her on her stomach, taking her from behind. I didn't waste a fucking second. Like I was possessed by her scent, defiance, and tight pussy, I couldn't stop myself. I pounded hard, pressing her cheek to the floor, and fucked her like a savage.

I was so close.

So was Ava.

She put a chokehold on my dick, squeezing so tightly I was right there. Ready to come. Her arms and legs trembled, forcing me to hold her up.

I gripped her black hair in my hand and yanked on it. "Cum on my cock."

The front door slammed and two sets of footsteps hit the tile in the entryway. On schedule, Dante strolled into the room with Vittoria Vitale.

"Nico," Ava whined. "You have…"

Guests.

All part of the plan.

So I held my brother and Vittoria's gaze and continued to fuck Ava. I slammed into her harder, my hand wrapped around her throat.

Vittoria folded her arms over her breasts and glared at me. Dante snickered, his gaze flicking between Ava and me.

Ava couldn't stop the orgasm rocking through her and screamed for me. Not when she was this close, right at the peak of her climax. Seconds later, I came inside her, completely fucking spent.

"You should have called first," I said to Dante.

Dante was happy to help when I asked him to bring Vittoria to my apartment. She wouldn't marry me if I weren't faithful.

And my heart belonged to Ava.

My older brother stood over us. "Did you forget Vittoria was coming here to talk about the wedding?"

Dante could carry on a conversation no matter what. Through sex, torture, digging fucking ditches to dump bodies. Anything. Nothing ever fazed my brother, though Vittoria looked pretty damn shocked.

I pulled out of Ava and shook my head at my brother. "Too much shit on my mind."

Dante's eyes narrowed at Ava. "Yeah? Looks like it."

After last night, merging with the Vitales was not an option. Although, if what we saw on Ava's birth certificate was true, that was another issue we would have to deal with later. But until we had the paternity test results, we wanted to keep the information to ourselves.

Vittoria chewed her lip, anger flaring in her eyes, but it wasn't sexy like when my girl did it. Looking at Vittoria after fucking a beauty like Ava made my skin crawl.

"You're disgusting, Nicodemus." Vittoria spat on the floor beside my hand. "I asked you if she was going to be a problem, and you lied to my face. I'm done." She stripped off the diamond ring and threw it at me. "The engagement is off."

Ava sat up and covered her tits, even though it did nothing to

162

hide her gorgeous body. I hooked my arm around Ava and lifted her off the floor.

"My father and brothers will hear about this." Vittoria shook her head, and her nose tipped up in disgust. "I don't want any part of this family or you." Then, she spun on her heels and walked away.

Dante snapped his fingers. "No, you don't. Get back here, Vittoria."

My ex-fiancee stopped at the entrance to the living room and angled her body to look at my brother. "You may have power over your family, but you don't control mine. And you never will."

Ava clung to my side, using my body to shield hers.

Dante strolled over to Vittoria and lowered his voice so I couldn't hear. He nodded for her to follow him, and then they were gone.

"What's going to happen?" Ava asked me.

I sat on a barstool and pulled her into my arms. "Remember when I said I would get out of the engagement?"

Her mouth widened in surprise. "You're sneaky. Why didn't you tell me this was part of your plan?"

"Because it needed to look real."

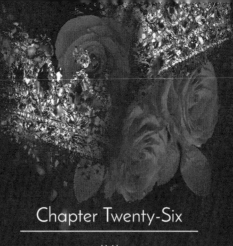

Chapter Twenty-Six

AVA

Nico was working from home, so I spent the day with him. My guys were afraid to leave me alone after the Vitales threatened another war because of me. So I spent most of the day on Nico's couch binge-watching Netflix.

Around dinnertime, my stomach rumbled, so I searched for Nico. I found him behind the desk, his suit jacket on the chair back, his long-sleeve shirt rolled up to his elbows. He clasped a pen, head down as he stared at a document.

"Are you working through dinner?" I stepped into the office. "I'm kinda hungry if you wanna eat with me."

He dropped the pen onto the desk and beckoned me with his finger. "*Vieni, passerotta.*"

Holding his gaze, I strolled to him in the cute red dress he'd picked out for me. My men spoiled me like a queen.

He hooked his arm around me and sat me on his lap. "What do you want to eat?"

I slid my arm across the back of his neck and smiled. "Surprise me."

Nico removed his cell phone from his pocket and ordered us a pizza and a bottle of red wine from room service.

"You've been in this office all day. What are you working on?"

"Legal stuff."

"That's vague." I laughed. "What kind of legal stuff?"

When I stared directly into his blue eyes, I completely lost myself in them. Everything about Nico was so beautiful. And yet, the darkness inside him was so ugly.

But I loved him.

"I'm going over a bill that will take money from the casinos. It can't pass. So it's my job to figure out if there's a way around it or if we needed to crack some skulls."

"You're looking for legal loopholes?"

He nodded to confirm. "It's not just the money the state will take from the casinos. The bill also affects how we run our business. It will create more roadblocks, making it harder to hide our less legitimate activities."

"Doesn't the state make more money if you do?"

"Yeah. But some people are convinced we're the problem with Atlantic City." Nico rolled his broad shoulders against the leather chair. "Probably true. But fuck em'."

"Has your dad said anything about the engagement to you?"

Nico sighed. "He's not happy with me. That's for fucking sure."

"What happens now that Vittoria canceled the engagement?"

"We'll be at war with the Vitales again. They have stronger ties to the Zabatino family, which means they'll come for us again."

I "slid my arm across his neck. "Johnny Z took some of Stefan's girls from the club."

He nodded. "Stefan got them back. But it's not the end with Johnny Z. He's been sending his associates to our casino to cheat."

"The card counters we watched... Were those Johnny Z's guys?"

"Probably." Nico turned me so I was sideways on his lap. "Dante broke their legs and sent them back to their boss."

My eyes widened. "Your brother is pretty violent."

"I'm no saint, baby." He rose from the chair, setting my feet on the floor. "I've killed a lot of men."

He clutched my shoulder and led me out of his office.

"How many people have you killed?"

Nico chuckled. "Why so interested in that?"

"I want to know more about you. Even the dark and dirty parts. Nothing about you scares me."

"I don't know," he confessed. "I lost count after my twentieth kill."

"Twenty?"

He grabbed my hand and led me down the hallway. "It's a lot more than twenty. I was maybe twenty-three when I stopped counting."

Nico was almost thirty.

Fuck.

"How old were you the first time?" I asked when we were sitting at the bar stools in the kitchen.

"Seventeen."

No emotion.

No regret.

The Nico I knew was different, yet he was also a cold-blooded killer.

"Did they deserve it?"

He nodded. "All of them. We don't kill innocents. Death is a means to an end, not something I enjoy."

"Dante does."

"My brother loves it."

Someone knocked on the front door.

"Wait here." Nico pulled a chair from the kitchen island for me to sit. "That's our food."

He returned a minute later with a box of pizza and a bottle of red wine. After Nico put the pizza on plates and poured two glasses of wine, he tipped his head at the living room.

"C'mon, I wanna relax. It's been a long fucking day."

I plopped onto the couch beside him and folded my slice in half, letting some of the grease drip onto the plate. We ate in silence, which was fine. Neither of us needed to speak to enjoy the other's company.

Midway through our meal, his cell phone rang.

"For fucks sake," he groaned as he looked at the screen and raised the phone to his ear. "What?"

I heard Dante curse at him in Italian.

Nico nodded. "Yeah. Be there in a minute." He stuffed the phone into his pocket and groaned. "Can't even enjoy a fucking meal without him calling me."

"Is everything okay?"

"Who fucking knows?"

Nico bent down to kiss me, stealing the air from my lungs. It didn't last long, but the effects of his touch left a lasting impression.

"Be a good girl for me." He ran his fingers through my long hair and gave me a peck. "I'll be back as soon as I can."

I stood on my tippy toes and wrapped my arms around his neck. "How long will you be gone?"

"I don't know. Watch a movie. Order whatever you want. Call the front desk and ask for Mrs. Destefano if you need anything."

Nico kissed me one last time, and then he was gone.

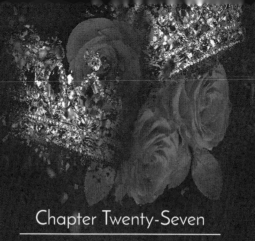

Chapter Twenty-Seven

ANGELO

F or most of my life, I didn't think much about Nico. He was
the golden boy and wasn't around much when I was
growing up. While he was off at college, I was here with my
brothers learning the family business. But he shocked the hell
out of me.

His single act of rebellion proved he wasn't a good boy
anymore.

He had balls.

About time.

I only wished I could have been there to see the look on Vittoria's face when Nico was fucking Ava on the floor.

Priceless.

Our father summoned us after he got the news from Paulie
that the wedding was off. Good fucking riddance to that stupid
family. Of course, neither of them were thrilled. Paulie was the
one pushing the marriage from the start. And for some idiotic
reason my dad went along with it.

Something was off about him lately.

Paulie was making more decisions for our dad, acting like the
boss, not his advisor. He was getting older, but he wasn't that
fucking old.

A few times, Dad started repeating himself, or even forgot

what he ate for dinner. Normal shit that he laughed off when we confronted him about it. Nico had suspected for a while that Dad wasn't okay. Even his mistress agreed. So when Dad suggested Nico marry a Vitale, he had to be losing his mind. That was the only explanation for his ridiculous plan.

We sat in his living room, waiting for him to speak. He'd been staring at each of us from the armchair and sipping scotch from the glass. Even at his age, he was still intimidating.

"Paulie spoke with Vincenzo Vitale," Dad said after a long pause. "The engagement is off."

Tell us something we don't know.

"I'm sorry, Papa. I know I screwed up." Nico rested his elbow on the arm of the couch and leaned closer to our dad. "But I—"

"I'm disappointed with you. We needed this marriage to unite our families, not start another war."

Dante even helped Nico end the engagement. None of us wanted to be attached to the Vitale family for the rest of our lives. That would have meant holidays and meals together. The few times I had to see Carlo were enough.

I wanted to kill that motherfucker.

Not be his brother-in-law.

"I have another way for us to settle the score with the Vitales." Dante removed a piece of paper from the inner pocket of his suit jacket and unfolded it. He handed it to our dad. "This will change Vincenzo's mind about another war."

We took turns reading the paternity results before we came over to our dad's penthouse.

Dad read the paper in disbelief, his eyes widening as he scanned the lab results. "Giancarlo isn't Ava's father." He looked at Dante. "How did you get this information?"

Dante set his glass on the coffee table and steepled his hands on his lap. "I found Ava's birth certificate in Giancarlo's safe. Someone crossed out his name and wrote Vincenzo Vitale. So Nico took one of Giancarlo's toothbrushes."

"And I got samples of her hair and saliva," I chimed.

He didn't want to know how I got the saliva, so I kept out

that part, laughing on the inside. Stefan smirked as our eyes met. Nico shook his head and chuckled.

"I had the samples analyzed," Dante said.

Dad leaned back in the chair, folding his hands on his lap as he stared out the patio doors. The sound of the Atlantic Ocean permeated every inch of the space. We grew up to that soothing sound that often comforted each of us.

"The marriage between Nico and Vittoria didn't work out," my dad said with a sly grin. "However, if this is true, Vincenzo has more than one daughter." His eyes moved to Dante and stayed there. "Dante, as my oldest, it's time for you to marry. And you will marry Ava."

Dante's eyes narrowed into slits. He looked frozen, as if he were unable to move.

Nico gasped. "But Dante doesn't even like Ava. He treats her like shit."

I begged to differ.

The special bracelet Dante had made for Ava's birthday said otherwise. He could act like he hate fucked her, but that was far from the truth. My older brother had it just as bad for Ava as the rest of us.

Dante tapped his long fingers on his knee, his expression unreadable. As usual, you couldn't tell what he was thinking. Even when Dante was angry, he hid his emotions well.

"I'll marry Ava if Dante doesn't want to," Stefan offered.

My twin was so in love with Ava it was written on his face. I felt things for her I didn't think I would ever feel for a woman. And Nico was obsessed with Ava and would have married her in a heartbeat.

But Dante?

"We don't know Vincenzo is Ava's father," Dante said calmly as if my dad asked him about the weather, not proposed marriage. "The test only ruled out Giancarlo. Anyone could have written Vincenzo's name on Ava's birth certificate."

"It will test positive for Vincenzo," Dad said with certainty, shifting his drink to his left hand. "Before Ava was born, Giancarlo suspected she wasn't his. He saw Francesca leaving the bathroom with Vincenzo at one of my parties. A month later, he told me Francesca was pregnant with Ava."

"That doesn't mean Vincenzo is her father," Nico pointed out.

"Giancarlo has unusually low testosterone," he told us between sips of his drink. "And an even lower sperm count. They tried to have children for years without success. Francesca was distraught, threatened to divorce Giancarlo because of it."

"Is that why he sent Ava's mother away?" Stefan asked.

Dad shrugged. "Francesca started drinking and popping pills after she had Ava. It only got worse as the years went by. Francesca gossiped about our family in public. Having her around was too much of a liability. So we locked her in an institution in California."

Nico puffed his cigar, the smoke billowing around his head. "I thought she was in rehab?"

Our father shook his head. "No, it's an asylum for the mentally ill. Giancarlo wanted Ava to believe her mom was someplace nicer. A spa for rich people."

"She thinks her mom chose to abandon her," Nico said with pain in his tone.

He knew what it was like to have an absentee mother. Cara handed over Nico and went back to Las Vegas to be a showgirl without a second thought. At least we didn't have to see her much growing up.

"It was for her benefit," Dad explained. "Francesca wasn't a perfect mother. Something inside her snapped after the pregnancy. Giancarlo kept her locked in the house, rarely allowed her to leave. And she took it out on Ava. Sending her away gave Ava a chance to learn from Giancarlo without her mother interfering."

Dante tugged on his tie as if it were suddenly too tight, and he couldn't breathe. "Are you sure about this marriage, Papa?"

Before he could respond, Paulie entered the room with his cell phone raised to his ear. "We'll be there," he muttered into the receiver and ended the call. He stopped beside my dad's chair and put his hand on his shoulder. "Salvatore, I have good news. Vincenzo and his sons have agreed to meet at a secure location to discuss compensation."

My dad handed him the DNA results. "I have a better idea."

Paulie took a moment to analyze the results. "Is this real?"

Dad told his advisor about Ava's birth certificate and explained how we obtained the results.

"What do you propose?"

He glanced up at Paulie. "Dante will marry Ava."

Our father's advisor folded the test results in half and stuffed them into his jacket pocket. "I'll make the necessary arrangements."

Chapter Twenty-Eight

DANTE

Being the underboss of the Boardwalk Mafia came with many responsibilities and a duty to my family. So when my father ordered me to marry Ava, I had no choice.

I gave Nico shit for having to marry Vittoria. We all made fun of him for being a good boy, the perfect son who never said no. By helping him end the engagement, I fucked myself.

A married man.

Me?

I still couldn't wrap my head around the events of the past two hours. We went from my father's penthouse to the secure location on Mississippi Ave. Another meeting to discuss marriage to a Vitale.

Ava Vitale.

Fuck.

If my dad was right, Ava was Vincenzo's daughter—the spawn of our enemy. That meant we didn't have to honor our deal with Ava on her birthday. Giancarlo wasn't her dad and, therefore, fair game.

I sat on my father's right side at a round booth at the back of Monviso, an Italian restaurant owned by a local chef. He was an ally of both families, which made it the perfect meeting place. It was well after hours, and we had the place to ourselves.

Angelo shifted beside me, tugging on his tie. He hadn't spoken much since we left the Portofino.

None of my brothers did.

Nico was at the Portofino, keeping an eye on Ava. After all the drama with the Vitales, we couldn't take any chances.

Someone had to stay with her.

So it had to be Pretty Boy.

Stefan tipped back a glass of scotch, surveying the bleak mood in the room. He was pissed about me getting to marry Ava. My little brother didn't need to say the words aloud for me to know. Both of the twins were annoyed about our father's decision.

Tough shit.

Paulie entered the dining room from the kitchen and set a plate of antipasto on the table. My brothers reached for the bread at once, knocking into each other. Angelo tapped Stefan's hand and took the first piece of bread. Even though Stefan was older by two minutes, Angelo was the aggressor. When they were kids, Angelo would push Stefan around until he got his way.

Nothing had changed.

Paulie took his place beside our father and leaned over to look at each of us. "Vincenzo is amenable to negotiation. I think we can come to an arrangement that benefits both families."

"Agreed." Dad sipped from his glass, eyeing his advisor from beneath his dark brows. "The marriage between Dante and Vittoria is a much better solution to war."

"You mean Ava, Papa," Angelo corrected.

"Huh?" He turned to look at Angelo. "Didn't I say that?"

"No." Angelo sighed. "You said Vittoria."

In his old age, our dad was getting softer. He wasn't interested in feuding with the other crime families in the city. Salvatore Luciano used to be a man people feared. And lately, he was becoming a different man.

Forgetful.

Weak.

That wasn't good for business.

If our enemies knew about his sudden memory loss, they would use it against us. So we had to present a solid, unified front. Either Paulie or I would do most of the talking.

Paulie tapped my dad on his arm. "It's okay, Sal. I'll handle the negotiations."

I raised my arm to check my watch. The Vitales should have arrived five minutes ago. They were fucking late.

I valued punctuality.

Those bastards were disrespecting us by making us wait. And after ten more minutes, the mood shifted. Angelo was getting antsy and drinking too much. Stefan played a game on his cell phone like a bored child.

"I'm done waiting," Dad said with anger in his tone. "No more negotiations."

A group of men in suits stormed into the dining room, wearing bandanas over their noses and mouths. The front door slammed behind them, bringing with them the summer heat.

"What the fuck?" Angelo grunted.

"Paulie, move," my dad shouted, since his advisor was the reason we couldn't get out from the table.

He didn't budge.

It was a setup.

Fuck.

I reached for my gun holstered on my chest. My brothers and father did the same. But before I could point and shoot, a bullet hit my chest. And then another. Pain tore through my body, spreading down my arms and back.

A bullet hit my father, tearing into his shoulder before one hit him in the chest. Angelo and Stefan ducked, holding up the table to shield us.

I pointed my gun over the top of the table and got off a round, shooting at anything that moved. Bullets sailed past my head and sank into the leather booth behind me.

Dad slumped to the side, clutching his chest. "Dante," he muttered, his eyes meeting mine, barely open.

I was in so much pain that it hurt to put my hand on his shoulder as he took his last breath.

No.

My eyelids fluttered, the pain taking over, making it impossible to stay awake. I blinked a few times and splayed my fingers over the bullet wounds on my chest. Blood bloomed through the white dress shirt, dripping onto my fingers and leaking onto the bench.

"I told you they would fall for it," Paulie said.

That fucking traitor.

Angelo and Stefan were injured beside me, leaning into each other. Dad was on his side, lifeless.

"Thanks for helping us out." A hand slapped Paulie's back. "Welcome to the family, Amato. You won't regret this."

Johnny Zabatino.

What the fuck?

That was the last I heard before I lost consciousness.

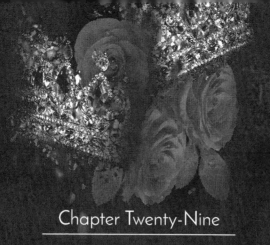

Chapter Twenty-Nine

NICO

Hours after my family left for the meeting, I sat in the living room with Ava. She bit her fingernails down to the skin, unable to sit still.

"Where are they?" Ava crossed her legs on the couch and turned to look at me. "They've been gone for too long."

I tried calling my family again and got voicemails. "I don't know, baby. But we'll find them."

Something was wrong.

They should have been home by midnight. And as the hours ticked by, I was growing more concerned. Even Paulie wasn't answering his cell phone.

I lifted Ava into my arms and put her on my lap. She slid her arm across my neck and kissed my lips.

"Are you telling me the truth, Nico?"

"Yes." I kissed her back. "I don't know why they're not answering their phones."

She sighed. "I have a bad feeling."

"I'm sure they're okay," I lied.

It didn't take much stress to stir up Ava's asthma. So I didn't want to worry her until I had more information.

I continued calling my brothers, father, and Paulie on rotation for another hour before someone knocked on my front door.

Holding Ava in my arms, I got up from the couch and set her on the floor. She followed me to the door.

When I swung it open, Paulie Amato stood on the other side. He had blood on his white dress shirt and streaks on his skin. There was a reason we had a private entrance to our penthouses.

"What the fuck happened?" I yanked on his arm and pulled him into the apartment. "Where is my dad? My brothers?"

"The Vitales didn't show." Paulie scrubbed a hand across his jaw. "A group of masked men took out your family."

Ava gasped. "What do you mean they took them out?"

His gaze shifted to Ava. "Dante is on life support. He may never wake from a coma."

"What?" Ava's hand flew to her mouth, tears streaming down her cheeks. "No. How about the twins?"

"They're in surgery."

"No, no, no...." Ava sobbed into her hands and screamed. "No, they're not allowed to die on me."

I held back the tears that pricked my eyes. Ava was a wreck and needed me to be her rock, even though I wanted to slump to the couch and cry with her.

"My dad?" I choked out, clearing the lump forming at the back of my throat.

Paulie shook his head. "I'm sorry, Nico. Unfortunately, Sal didn't make it."

"I need to see them." Clinging to my arm, Ava tugged on my suit jacket. "Take me to the hospital."

"It's not safe," Paulie said with caution in his tone. "The Vitales picked off your family one by one. If you leave the penthouse, you risk getting whacked." He tipped his head at Ava. "And there's no guarantee for her safety either. This attack was an act of war."

"No," Ava cried. "We have to see them. I want to be there when Dante wakes up."

"If he wakes up," Paulie said with a grim expression. "The doctor didn't sound optimistic."

"What about the twins?"

Paulie shrugged. "They won't know until after they get out of surgery."

His words had a bite to them as if he thought they might not make it through the surgery.

"You have to step up as the interim head of the family." Paulie patted my shoulder and squeezed. "The men can't go to war without a leader."

Technically, I wasn't allowed to be a made man because I wasn't one hundred percent Italian descent. But my dad made an exception for me. Some of his men rebelled back then, and now that he was gone, I doubted they would accept me as their leader.

Dante needed to wake up.

They respected him.

"I need to see my dad," I told him.

His eyebrows rose. "Didn't you hear me, kid? He's dead."

I hated when he called me kid.

Folding my arms over my chest, I took a deep breath to still my nerves. "I'm not doing anything until I see my family. Dead or alive."

Read the conclusion to the series.

Learn more about the series at JillianFrost.com

The Frost Society

Welcome to The Frost Society!

You have been chosen to join an elite secret society for readers who love dark romance books.

When you join The Frost Society, you will get instant access to all of my novels, bonus scenes, and digital content like new-release eBooks and serialized stories. You can also get discounts for my book and merch shop, exclusive book boxes, and so much more.

Learn more at JillianFrost.com

Also by Jillian Frost

Princes of Devil's Creek

Cruel Princes

Vicious Queen

Savage Knights

Battle King

Read the series

Boardwalk Mafia

Boardwalk Kings

Boardwalk Queen

Boardwalk Reign

Read the series

Devil's Creek Standalone Novels

The Darkest Prince

Wicked Union

Read the books

For a complete list of books, visit JillianFrost.com.

Get to know Jillian Frost

Get early-access, bonus content, and more of the characters you
love when you become a Fangirl

Join Jillian Frost on Patreon

Watch Jillian's latest videos on TikTok
@jillianfrostbooks

Become part of a reader community when you join Jillian's
private Facebook group called Frost's Fangirls

Check out the latest teasers and updates on Jillian's Instagram
@jillianfrostbooks

About the Author

Jillian Frost is a dark romance author who believes even the villain deserves a happily ever after. When she's not plotting all the ways to disrupt the lives of her characters, you can usually find Jillian by the pool, soaking up the Florida sunshine.

Learn more about Jillian's books at JillianFrost.com

Made in the USA
Columbia, SC
08 June 2023

17798226R00121